LUPE WONG
WON'T DANCE

LUPE WONG WON'T DANCE

by Donna Barba Higuera

Lantern
Paperbacks

This is a Lantern Paperback
Published by Levine Querido

www.levinequerido.com • info@levinequerido.com
Levine Querido is distributed by Chronicle Books, LLC

Library of Congress Control Number: 2019957009
ISBN 978-1-64614-160-9
Printed and bound in China

First Lantern Paperback Edition: June 2022
First Printing

FOR MY SOPHIA
WHO'S HANDLED CONFLICT,
ADVERSITY (AND SQUARE
DANCING) WITH GRACE,
KINDNESS, AND HUMOR

CHAPTER 1

My gym shorts burrow into my butt crack like a frightened groundhog. Note to self: remember shorts from home so you don't have to wear scratchy school loaners ever again. I can fix this. I pull up my kneepads, adjust my wristbands, and tighten my ponytail with a yank. Ready for battle, a.k.a. seventh-grade spring P.E.

Half a cheek hanging out, I glance around the locker room to make sure the coast is clear. I casually place one foot up on the bench and make a stealth grab, yanking my underwear down.

Samantha Pinkerton slams her locker so loud the entire room of girls looks in her direction. "Find anything good up there, Lupe?" She laughs and half the class snickers with her.

I almost respond with, "Yeah, your mom," but stop myself at the last possible second.

Samantha takes a step toward me and puts her nose inches from mine.

"Oh, yeah?" I say instead. This time the words are out before I can help it.

Samantha scrunches her face and scratches her temple, my comeback obviously stunning her into confusion. My best friend, Andy, cringes behind Samantha. Smack talk is not one of my strong points.

Coach Solden's whistle pierces the air. "Guadalupe Wong . . . Samantha Pinkerton!" Arms folded over her chest, she takes up the entire doorway of her office. "Anything you care to share with us?"

I clench my teeth and shake my head. I can't risk getting points off. I need to ace this class.

Samantha's voice is suddenly as sweet as her fruity body spray. "Just admiring Lupe's shorts, Coach Solden."

"Well, do it after class," Coach says, motioning for Samantha to get in line.

Samantha squints her eyes toward mine in some sort of staring standoff, but I can only focus on the cartoon salmon on the front of her shirt giving a thumbs-up. Someone forgot to tell the kid who designed the school mascot that Sammy Sockeye should have fins, not fingers. Samantha slithers into line behind me.

"Oh, yeah?" she says, mimicking me under her breath.

Thank God Andy is with me this quarter. "Ignore her," she mutters calmly from the next spot in line, shooting me a glance.

"I can bring you my extra soccer shorts tomorrow." Andy's mom has probably made sure she has four pairs to "ensure her academic success." To go with her new laptop and private tutoring.

I crack my knuckles in front of me. "Nope. I got this. I won't forget mine again."

We wait in a row to shuffle into the gymnasium for basketball or volleyball or whatever unit we have now. Coach wheels a TV out from the equipment closet in the back of the locker room. "No one moves; no one talks." She pushes the cart toward the swinging door.

"Wait, something's wrong," I say, watching Coach walk into the gym without a single ball.

Andy's voice sounds like it's rolling its eyes. "I know, I know . . ." She makes a mouth puppet with her hand, trying to imitate my voice. "Kids with long arms should be able to wear shorts to their wrists instead of fingertips . . . It shouldn't be a girl's responsibility to worry about how our clothing might distract boys . . ." She moves her hand puppet to make its mouth extra wide. "Aaaaand there should be a separate bubble under race for people of Chinacan or Mexinese descent . . ."

"Well, there should be!" I say. "You have a bubble for Black. Why should I have to *Choose One Bubble* or *Other*? Why should anyone?"

Most of my causes don't get further than a strongly worded letter to the principal. Andy shrugs.

"But that's not what I'm talking about," I go on, biting my lower lip. Co-ed P.E. is the one subject I should dominate. With everything but jump rope in the second grade, I've been on the boys' team. "Did you notice the TV? What if we have to learn some antique sport, like ... the one with mini tennis rackets and the plastic snow-cone thing?"

"It's called a shuttlecock," Andy giggles, and her dark curls bob up and down.

"Very funny, Andy. I really need this A," I say.

"I know you do. And that *really* is what it's called," she replies. "C'mon, you're the best in this class—you know you can handle anything. You'll be pitching cans of corn or whatever you call it to Fu Li in no time."

I've already filled Andy in on my uncle's promise. If I get straight As, my Uncle Hector, who works for the Mariners, is taking me to meet Fu Li Hernandez, the first Asian/Latino pitcher in the major leagues. If Fu Li can be the first Chinacan guy to pitch in the majors, maybe I can be the first Mexinese girl to throw a no-hitter.

Did I mention that baseball is life?

I've worked hard to get back on track and have As in the rest of my classes. I bite on the inside of my cheek thinking of Coach Solden and some new game risking my chance to meet Fu Li. Besides making it to the majors someday, I don't think I've ever wanted something so bad in my life.

Coach Solden returns to the locker room and flicks the fluorescent lights on and off. The last few stragglers jump into line. She lifts the whistle dangling down her chest and blows four short blasts, like she's leading an army troop out into battle.

Her shorts are riding up her butt more than mine, but she doesn't seem to care. She marches us into the gym where a group of twenty boys are already waiting.

My friend Niles waves at me from the line. I wave back and smile, but then he holds up his hand and mimics flipping on Doctor Who's Sonic Screwdriver, our signal for "we gotta talk" (and it's a "the-universe-is-in-danger" sort of emergency).

We have a half second before class starts, so I point toward a spot in between the boys and girls that's somewhat blocked from Coach's sight, and we break out of formation to meet up.

Samantha snicker-snorts and points at us.

"Hey, Lupe!" Niles says, letting out a breath.

I huddle up next to him for privacy. "What's up?"

A few of Samantha's friends follow along and start giggling at us too.

No way I'm letting this pass. I let a tiny one ooze out, a Silent But Deadly. *Three . . . two . . .*

Fumes fill the air. "Ewwww!" Samantha says. "I swear, it wasn't me," she whispers to her friend Claire.

I'm relishing my successful SBD bombing mission, so I lose focus and don't remain as still as I should. A fresh cloud billows up.

Niles shakes his head at me. "Really? I'm right here too."

"Sorry," I whisper. "Collateral damage."

He nods and stares past me toward the rafters, which makes it easier for him to have conversations, especially if he's a little stressed. I lean in even closer. "Listen, I've noticed something wrong."

Coach reprimands a straggler on the other side of the gym and the class starts to quiet down. We don't have much time. "I've noticed it too. Let's see what she's got and talk after class?"

"But this is huge," he whispers back and motions toward the TV. "Coach has never not started a class bouncing a ball, or tossing a ball, or juggling balls . . ."

Niles hates change as much as I do. I glance at Coach, who's now spinning the TV remote in her hand like it's a bat. "I know, I know," I mutter, allowing a little bit of my own worry to creep in. "What do you think? Maybe she's going to show us a new sport?"

"I guess . . ."

Coach turns to face us, still spinning the remote. "In line, Foster."

"Hurry. Line up," I whisper. "Before she makes us do push-ups or something."

Once back in our spots, I hold out a pretend Sonic Screwdriver and close its top, indicating we've at least acknowledged the emergency. Niles nods back.

Samantha is still gagging on my innard fumes so she can't be annoyed by our signals this time.

Coach Solden claps her hands, taking advantage of the lull in activity. "I have an announcement, everyone! Gather round."

She motions to the cart holding the TV. My stomach feels like the inside of a bouncy house.

Forty seventh graders move at once. A gentle wind of eighty shoes and armpits fills my nostrils.

Coach Solden scans the crowd, then scans back the other way. Her eyes lock on mine. I'm about to panic, but she's on to the next victim. One by one, she's making eye contact with a few of us. By the shuffling and fidgeting of the kids she's singling out, her laser stare pattern seems to be focused on the athletic kids. My catcher on the baseball team last year, Blake, looks over and arches his eyebrows just like he does every time the third hitter in the lineup is up to bat.

Coach Solden then makes her signature move, tucking in her one-size-too-small shirt into her two-sizes-too-small gym shorts. This might be even worse than I thought. My palms break out in a sweat. She presses play on the remote.

The TV screen lights up. Men and women are standing in a circle. The men have on jeans and checkered shirts, and the ladies are wearing matching puffy skirts bloated out like a Pinterest cupcake fail. I think I'm going to puke up my lunch. They're paired off, holding hands.

The screech of fiddles echoes through the gym.

A guy with a Southern accent wails in a scratchy twang.

"If it hadn't been for Cotton-Eyed Joe
I'd been married a long time ago

7

Where did you come from, where did you go?
Where did you come from, Cotton-Eyed Joe?"

It's like a bizarre hillbilly rap. Arm in arm, the people clomp around like trotting donkeys.

Coach Solden taps her foot and claps her hands to the song. She's about a half beat off, and her hips are wiggling from side to side. It's eerily similar to the time my mom insisted on teaching all my friends the Macarena at my birthday party. Even though I silently beg the universe to make it end, just like with my mom, Coach isn't stopping either.

Blake looks at me like he got lemon juice in his mouth. Zola Fimple covers her eyes. Marcus, our number-two pitcher in the rotation behind me, nerves up and makes a gagging noise. How do grown-ups not know how embarrassing they are? Finally, the music stops and Coach bows to an imaginary partner, just like the dancers on the video do to their real partners.

She hits stop on the remote. It takes her a few seconds to catch her breath. My mouth and the mouths of everyone in the room drop wide open as Coach's words echo out.

"Welcome to this quarter's curriculum, class!"

CHAPTER 2

I've never associated the inside of a gym with such horror. There has to be a way to make it stop. Fu Li Hernandez wouldn't be caught dead square dancing. Dancing belongs in nightclubs and ballet studios, not a gym. And square dancing belongs somewhere far away where it can't embarrass anyone, like the 1800s.

We spend the remaining twenty minutes of P.E. watching different versions of the same routine. I'm clenching my toes inside my shoes the entire time. I glance down the line. Most faces are aghast, like they just saw their grandma in her underwear. Except Carl Trondson's mouth is slightly ajar and his eyes are closed. Is he seriously sleeping through this horror? And Gordon Schnelly, he's actually tapping his foot along with the music! Each square dance starts with a different man or woman, all with Southern accents, wailing, "If it hadn't been for Cotton-Eyed Joe, I'd been married a long time ago."

When the women sing, Cotton-Eyed Joe sounds like even more of a jerk. What had he done to them that they all would've been married and happy if he hadn't come along? Bad enough that Cotton-Eyed Joe had ruined their lives—now he's trying to ruin mine.

Finally, the torture of the music and watching Coach Solden jog around flailing her arms and legs is over. But some things you can't unsee.

"By the way." Coach gives us a wink. "Lace up your dancing shoes. We start tomorrow."

An icy shiver runs up my spine. A low groan echoes through the gym. I think I hear someone clap, but it must be my imagination. Shoulders sagging, we retreat to the locker rooms.

Andy and I change quickly and head to wait outside the boys' locker room.

Blake walks out wearing our team's Issaquah Select baseball jersey and gives me a fist bump. "Hey, Lupe. How's the arm?"

I make a muscle, and Blake leans in squinting. I chuck him on the shoulder and we both start laughing.

He walks away and Andy rolls her eyes. "You guys are dorks," she says.

As the last of the boys stream out, I arch my head around the corner. "Niles! We're not going to prom!"

"Sorry!" he yells back.

Gordon Schnelly beats him out. Gordon is sweating even though we didn't do anything.

The two-minute warning bell rings. Niles walks out tying his "Annelids Unite! Save the Giant Palouse Earthworm!" sweatshirt around his waist. I might be what my mom calls "a social justice warrior," but Niles is a huge advocate for our region's endangered species. Unfortunately for Niles, the Pacific Northwest has some bizarre endangered animals.

"And just so you know, if you *were* trying to take me to prom, I wouldn't come out at all." He motions over his head for us to catch up, like we're the ones who've made us late for our last class of the day.

We speed walk away from the gym and toward the main building. Other kids run past in the opposite direction. When the halls come into view, Andy, Niles, and I exchange a glance. Extra crammed halls mean extra danger.

In elementary school, Niles had Mr. Nguyen as his special ed. teacher back when we didn't rotate classrooms. Now Niles goes to the Learning Resource Center (a.k.a. LRC) twice a week with Mr. Lambert, or when he, his mom, or a teacher requests it. Niles is on the autism spectrum, so they've worked his schedule so he doesn't have to spend too much time in the halls. But our last class of the day takes us right down the main hallway. And this is one of those days that makes me nervous.

I lock elbows with Niles on one side and Andy on the other. The school hallways are outside, so even when it's barely sprinkling (which is nearly every day in the Northwest), everyone rushes more. Kids jostle past one another like salmon in the river by our school. So our janky school mascot is appropriate for more than one reason. Someone even painted the halls mud and algae colors to make us feel like Sammy Sockeye too.

"Let's go," Andy says, just before we plunge in. We huddle close together and ease into the main hall.

A mechanical pencil falls out of Andy's unzipped bag about two seconds in and I grab her before she bends down. "What are you doing?" I squeak out. I hand her one of my pencils and keep things moving. "Let it go. You could end up with a concussion or lose a limb."

Andy stares back longingly as her pencil disappears in a twister of legs and feet.

Even though my brother, Paolo, routinely threatens to "return me to the zoo where my parents found me," he liked me enough to warn me about the mortal dangers of the halls before I started middle school. "If you die, more food for me. But if you want to live through middle school, keep moving, and, never, ever stop to pick up something you've dropped."

It's like a *Fast and the Furious* speed track, but half the people are racing in the wrong direction. On the first day of middle school, Gordon Schnelly ran head-on into a kid with a scoliosis brace and chipped one front tooth and lost the other. He never did find the tooth that flew off the cement path into the mud sludge.

I dodge two chatty girls who are not respecting the passing

lanes. When I see a quick break in the traffic, I whip around to face Niles and Andy and start walking backward.

"So, what do you think our plan should be?" I ask.

"Plan for what?" Niles says. Andy also looks puzzled.

"Weren't you there?" My voice is higher than usual. "To get rid of square dancing. I'd do almost anything else than bounce around like a doofus wearing a picnic blanket. Besides, P.E. is not the place for dancing."

Andy rolls her eyes. "I see a new cause coming."

Niles executes an impossible last-minute side step before he gets pummeled by a sprinter. "Would you rather eat raw maggot puke or learn the dance?" he says.

"Raw maggot puke for sure," I say.

I come up with the two most disgusting things I can at the moment. "Would you rather dance with Samantha or eat locker room drain hair?" I ask.

"Drain hair, not even close," Niles answers, and we burst out laughing.

Andy scoffs. "That's not really helpful, you guys."

Niles and I can't get enough of our "would you rathers"; they've always been our thing. But they're not really Andy's. Between her mom's mandated after-school computer coding and Colloquial Japanese for International Business classes, Andy probably doesn't have room left in her brain for pondering much of anything else. And right now, she's probably right. We have more important things to focus on.

"So how are we getting rid of square dancing?" I ask.

"Is this because of your grades thing?" Andy asks.

I shrug. Never mind that I still have As in math, language arts, and social studies. But a little mind-wandering in the past year led to a B or two. Now every aunt, uncle, and second cousin who expects you to be the first doctor in the family knows about it, and "knows you'll do better next year, Lupe!"

"I still don't get why your Uncle Hector won't just take you to meet Fu Li. He knows how important it is to you."

"It makes sense," Niles answers. "He knows exactly how to make Lupe work harder."

Andy nearly trips on a rogue water bottle but keeps walking. "Well, I don't think square dancing will be that bad. I bet your uncle will buckle anyway."

Andy has no idea what she's talking about. She's never met my Uncle Hector either. His motto is, "We're Mexi-cans, not Mexi-can'ts." And as cheesy and stupid as it sounds, he's not joking. Plus, Uncle Hector apparently told Fu Li about my grades slipping. Fu Li even gave Uncle Hector a handwritten note to give to me: *Anyone can pitch a good inning, pitching an entire good game takes character. Work hard so I can meet you!*

I'm not even sure what his note means, but Fu Li must have a Mexican uncle too.

"No, I think he'll hold me to it," I say. "I have to talk to Coach Solden after school. I only have one hour to figure out how I'm going to convince her to eliminate square dancing forever."

"Like I said, she has a new cause." Andy makes a hand puppet.

14

"Square dancing leads to foot fungus and toe jam," she mimics my voice again. "It must be abolished before the entire seventh grade class is footless." She winks at me and takes a sharp left into her social studies class.

Even though the halls are thinning out, it's still about as loud as it was on the field when Fu Li threw a no-hitter two seasons ago. Niles motions toward our science class and we both hustle to get out of the chaotic hallway. Burnt chemical smell greets us as we walk in.

Niles and I barely make it into our seats before the bell rings. Somehow we got teamed with Gordon Schnelly Spring quarter in our lab group. Gordon insists on wearing his protective goggles even though we haven't started any experiments yet. He spouted off something about remnant toxic fumes and his corneas on the first day.

Gordon speaks with the lisp he's had since that fateful day with the scoliosis brace. "Howth it going guyth?" Sometimes he's difficult to understand, but luckily Niles speaks Gordonese, and I'm learning. We've never really spent much time with Gordon before, but if he's going to be our lab partner for the rest of the year, we need to figure each other out.

"Lupe hates square dancing," Niles says.

"I, for one, am looking forward to it." Gordon sits up taller.

Now I know who clapped back in P.E. during the announcement. How can someone actually like square dancing?

"My grandma says we make perfect dance partners, both

15

being single and all," Gordon continues, making a little dance move. "She also says I have natural rhythm." He looks more like a seal swallowing a fish, but I don't say anything.

Niles nods approvingly. "Music and rhythm are well docu—" Niles's eyes suddenly go wide. He points to an emblem in the center of Gordon's shirt that looks sort of like arched wings with a Christmas tree star in the center. "Jedi?"

Gordon claps his hands together like he just got the top gift on his birthday list. "*Star Wars* fan?"

"Trekkie," Niles counters. He makes a gesture that looks like some of his fingers are stuck together in a hand cramp.

"Interstellar game on, Niles." Gordon narrows his eyes in challenge, for what I'm pretty sure is some sort of galactic turf war. But they both look pretty happy.

Mr. Lundgren, our science teacher, starts speaking and the mumbling around the classroom stops. His voice never shifts out of the low tractor gear of monotone. "Today class, we will be studying the miracle of the Krebs cycle."

I pull out a piece of paper. Instead of writing *Krebs Cycle* like everyone else, I write *Square Dancing*, then draw a circle around the word and a diagonal line marking over the word. I put my head on the desk. Years of chemicals are probably seeping into my brain. I don't care. It seems hopeless. I peek at Gordon who's already drawing arrows coming into and off a circle on his paper. Letters and gibberish go into the circle and more gibberish comes off.

Niles pats my arm. "Want me to take our notes today instead?"

16

I look up to see him grinning. Growing up four houses down from mine, Niles and I have always teamed up, from selling lemonade to buy me a new glove, to painting address numbers on curbs so we could pay for his latest graphic novel.

But today was my turn to take notes.

"Would you?" I ask.

Niles answers by taking out his notebook and hurrying to catch up with the rest of the class.

Mr. Lundgren starts drawing the same picture on the whiteboard that Gordon has already finished. While Niles takes our real notes, I pretend.

—Square dancing is not a sport. (Use Olympics as example if necessary.)

—Handholding is unhygienic.

—Look for stats on deaths during square dancing.

—Square dancing is

The lights in the room are on a motion detector, and turn off every so often during the lecture, interrupting my thoughts. Mr. Lundgren waves an arm at sloth speed to make them go back on. But after forty-five minutes, I've only come up with a few bullet points.

Still, I grip the paper tight in my hands so I don't lose it in the after-school scuffle. After the final bell rings, I wait in the doorway for Niles to finish talking to Gordon about something.

As we walk toward the bus, I review my talking points in

quiet murmurs. Should I present my list to Coach Solden now, or go home and create a PowerPoint for emphasis?

But if she's making us dance tomorrow . . .

When we're almost to the bus, my hands suddenly break out in a sweat again. "Niles, I gotta go talk to Coach now. Will you wait for me?"

Niles shrugs. "Sure. I'll let my mom know we're walking home." He's already pulling out his phone. "I might pop into LRC and ask Mr. Lambert what he thinks of the square dancing thing. If I'll need anything if I decide to do it. Come find me in the library when you're done."

I pick up my pace. The outside door to her office has a "Coach S" plaque under a little window near the top.

I put my ear to the door. Coach is singing along to "Dancing Queen" by ABBA. I knock and wait.

"Come in," she says.

I open the door and poke my head in. The aroma from years of coffee and musty P.E. gear fills the room. "Hey Coach."

She turns the volume down on the music. "Lupe." She motions for me to sit.

Painted on the wall behind her are the sit-up, pull-up, and standing long jump records for our school. University of Washington purple-and-gold pennants plaster over any empty space like wallpaper, and a stuffed Huskies mascot stares back at me from the front of her desk.

I sit across from her and try to act casual.

"Can I help you with something?" she asks.

18

I hold my chin and stare out her window toward the cafeteria like I've seen professors and philosophers do in movies.

"Spit it out," she says.

I drop my hand to my lap and face her. "Why didn't you mention at the beginning of the year that we'd have to dance in P.E.?"

"You do know it's standard curriculum, right?" she says.

I lift my hands, palms up. "No."

"Yes. Since 1938, the Sockeye Salmon of Issaquah Middle School have enjoyed a lively square dance." Teeth bucked out, Coach rocks her arms in front of her like a square-dancing squirrel. "Official state dance of twenty-four states in our union."

The pit in my stomach grows to the size of that squirrel's entire winter nut supply. How can I fight something nearly half the country has been brainwashed into?

"But . . . this is *physical* education," I say.

She folds her hands in front of her like she's in a business meeting. "It is. And, I think if you do a little research, you'll find that square dancing is a standard part of P.E. curriculum across our great nation."

This is going in the wrong direction. I need to strike. "Didn't you take some sort of P.E. teacher oath to test our actual athletic ability?"

Coach's cheeks turn a little red. I hope it's just from a busy day of jiggling around. "Physical education is just as much about coordination and willingness to learn something new as it is about sports. And trust me, it's a workout." She still has beads of

19

sweat on her brow and I realize she must've had another class right before this.

I glance down at my list. "Is square dancing even a sport? I mean, it's not in the Olympics, is it?"

"Some might argue ping-pong and sailing shouldn't be Olympic sports, but they are." She leans in. "By the way, baseball is currently *off* the list in the Olympics."

Heat runs up the back of my neck. I need to sidestep that revelation completely. I clear my throat. "Have you considered the hygiene aspect—"

Her laugh startles me. "This coming from the girl who holds the snot-rocket distance record," she says.

I wring my hands together, paper clenched between my fists. The words *stats on deaths* are crinkled. My list is toast.

Not only are my arguments completely shut down, Coach isn't taking me seriously at all.

I stare behind her at the school records. You can still see where they painted over *Becky Solden* under *Pull-ups*, and where *Guadalupe Wong* replaces it.

"But you have to know this is wrong, Coach. Jocks like us—"

"That's enough, Lupe." Her lips tighten together like a bear trap. She straightens up in her seat. "Sometimes we have to do things that are uncomfortable. Besides, it will build your character." She lowers her voice to almost a whisper. "I'll even let you in on a little secret. Spring quarter is special." Her voice is gaining strength. "The best dancers not only earn As, but a select few perform in front of the school for the Issaquah Salmon Days assembly." She claps her hands together. "Isn't that grand!"

I go to swallow and there's no spit. I can't think of anything much worse than dancing in front of the school.

"Work hard and you could be one of the eight students from your section to get this honor," she says.

"Honor?" I cough out.

She stands and opens the door.

"But Coach. What if—"

"Don't worry, Lupe," she calls back. "I'm sure you have what it takes to make a marvelous do-si-do-er."

CHAPTER 3

Niles pulls the striped rock we found the first week of second grade out of his backpack. Speaking of his backpack, it looks about twenty pounds heavier after his stop in the school library. Just like all other days we walk home, he drops the rock in front of me and I get the first kick. I kick it back to his side. "Would you rather have spider babies inside your nostrils or square dance?" I ask.

Niles shudders. "I'll take square dancing."

"Really?"

"Before spider babies? Yeah." Niles doesn't miss a beat, kicking it back to my side about five feet ahead of me. "Dog-poop-stuffed Oreo or square dance?"

That one makes me crack a grin. "You could even double stuff it."

I stop at my driveway.

We could go on for hours.

"Thanks for walking with me today."

"No problem." He picks up the rock and puts it in his front zipper pocket for next time.

"*Doctor Who* after dinner?" We have a regular Monday night meeting. It may or may not involve us sneaking some of his dad's Chunky Monkey ice cream then a post-game wrap-up of the episode.

"Uhhh, can't tonight," he says.

"Little Dragons?" I ask. Niles has a job instructing the three-to-five-year-olds martial arts class at his dojo. He normally teaches on Saturdays, but maybe they have belt testing tonight or something.

"No. I sort of made other plans today, but I promise to watch it before bed so we can talk about it tomorrow."

This is unusual, but I guess a recap is better than nothing. "Okay."

He waves over his head. As he walks away, I'm left wondering what in the universe can be more important than a *Doctor Who* Monday.

Our next-door neighbor, Delia, is sitting on the ground pruning her catnip when I walk by. She uses it to attract the cat she "adopted" (even though Fletcher technically belongs to the Nuñez family down the street). "Well hello, Lupe," she calls out to me. A smudge of mud streaks across her forehead, and reading glasses on the top of her head hold back hair wilder than her rosemary bush. "How are your studies going?"

I stop and smile. Why hadn't I thought of it? Not only is Delia a good listener when I need to vent, she's one of the best supporters I've had for my campaigns, *and* she's a child psychologist. She's a triple threat.

"Delia, don't you believe if teachers mislead students regarding curriculum, it could lead to trust issues in their adult life?" I ask.

Delia stops to ponder, holding a garden hose in one hand and "her cat" in the other. "Mmmh." I calculated once that our thirty-seconds-a-day exchanges, which started in kindergarten, will amount to almost $3,000 in free advice by the time I leave for college. "I suppose so. I guess it would depend on—"

"Thanks, Delia!" I walk quickly toward my house before she changes her mind. I glance back and she winks and gives me a thumbs up before turning back to her plants.

When I unlock the front door, I'm immediately fume-blasted with what can only be another Crock-Pot concoction. By the odor, Mom made some sort of beef and cumin. Hopefully, albondigas soup.

I go to the kitchen and lift up the glass lid. Not albondigas. I'm pretty sure the green sludge inside has some sort of squash that isn't meant to be slow-cooked for seven hours.

Since no one is home, I stop in the hallway at the picture of my dad, the one with him holding up a Dungeness crab on the fishing boat where he worked. It's one of those things I only do when I'm alone. My dad died a few years ago, and it's been long enough where I think I'm not supposed to miss him so much. But I can't help myself when no one is around.

I stare at his smile. The tiny lines at the corners of his eyes are one of the things I see in the picture but don't remember in real life. I rest my cheek on his face. The glass is cold. I know it's a little creepy because he died the very next day on that same boat. But still.

I'd give anything for one of our "signature secret handshakes," where he'd pretend he was going to high-five me, but would miss and pull me into a bear hug.

The glass against my cheek isn't warm like his chest.

And the picture doesn't smell like coffee and rain.

Dad's smile is even bigger in the picture above the crab photo. It's one of him playing baseball. He was good enough to make it to the minors, and though he had to stop when he and Mom had me and Paolo, he still played for the Everett AquaSox when he wasn't working on a ship. I wonder if a small part of him ever hoped he'd return to it for real.

I can't get my cheek high enough to reach that photo, though, even on tiptoe. It's been almost two years and I'm starting to forget things about Dad. But I do remember what he said when I was the first girl to make the Issaquah Select Little League team. "If there's something you're passionate about, don't ever settle for less."

Maybe my causes aren't exactly what he meant. But I'll never settle for something less than what I want.

Along with the pictures of my dad, our hallways are lined with calaveras art and little Chinese village paintings. Grandma Wong gives my mom the Chinese ones, even though none of us know what the brushstroke words mean. Mom's not going to let Grandma Wong outdo her culture in her own home, though—she has a framed Mayan calendar, and when the world didn't end like the calendar said it would, she moved it to the bathroom that already looks like it's right out of an Azteca restaurant.

I make a pit stop and hang my backpack in my room. Fu Li's rookie card is framed next to the hook. Dad's skin was darker, but they even sort of look alike. I close my eyes and imagine for a second throwing with Fu Li, and him giving me a high five.

I have to get rid of the stupid dance and get my A in P.E. so I can make this happen.

I put on my M's hat and grab my glove. My pitching net has a cutout strike zone with a mesh pocket behind it. The pocket fits around thirty baseballs, so three times in a row I fill the pocket with twenty-seven balls. Once I hit the zone eighty-one times (or if Mom gets home and yells for me to come in), I quit. I know it's not the real thing, but if I do it three times a week, I can pitch over a thousand perfect games by the time I'm in the majors. That's almost a hundred thousand strikes.

Sweat is dripping down my neck by the time I'm on seventy-six and Paolo walks out. He sits on the back porch, his jeans hiked halfway up his shins. He got his growth spurt this summer so he started his freshman year in high-waters. "Thirteen! Forty-two! Twenty-three!"

I ignore him. "Seventy-seven." I wipe my forehead and knock out the remaining four strikes.

The rattle of Mom's loose muffler echoes from the front of the house.

I sprint toward the house and Paolo's arm flies out like a broomstick. I hurdle over his arm and laugh. "Ha!" Looking back, I trip over the threshold of the door and almost can't recover.

I'm throwing cold water over my face in the kitchen sink by the time Mom walks in, and drops her purse on the counter. A crusty purple spot, suspiciously the exact hue of the homemade playdough she was making the night before, dots her shirt, and the hook of one of her earrings dangles dangerously close to falling out of her earlobe.

"Hey little one." Mom gives me a quick squeeze.

I reach up and slide her earring back into place. "Hey."

She walks over to the Crock-Pot. Lifting the lid, she winces. "Well, it smells good anyway." She lifts my hat like she did the Crock-Pot lid and takes a whiff. "Can't say the same. Go clean up and be back in ten," she says. Paolo and I both run for Azteca, but he wins. After a quick scrubdown, we're both back at the dinner table as my mom starts serving.

We each squeeze into our chairs in the kitchen nook. Dad's chair against the wall is still pulled out like he might show up any minute. We might gain valuable space if we moved Dad's chair out and shoved the table against the wall, but no one's brought it up even once, so I think we all prefer to leave Dad's chair right where it is and deal with the tiny kitchen.

Mom bows her head. "Paolo?"

His voice has about as much feeling as an email. "Thank you, God, for all that we have. Bless this interesting food to our bodies. And please help Lupe with her cleanliness so she can be next to you or whatever the saying thing says. Amen."

Mom sighs and sticks her fork in what looks like olive-colored jerky. "So, how was everyone's day?"

"Well," I say before Paolo can beat me. "You aren't going to believe what they're trying to pull in P.E."

"Yes, Becky Solden already called me," she says.

"She what?!" It's part of the punishment for having a parent who's also a teacher. Even worse, Mom teaches kindergarten at the local elementary school, so there's a decent chance she's had nearly every teacher's kid in her class at some point. I didn't stand a chance. They all know each other. Talk in class . . . Mom knows. Only read the first half of *Anne of Green Gables* then accidentally Google the ending of *Anne of Avonlea* instead for your book report . . . Mom knows.

"Coach Solden only wants you to be successful. I've neglected you in the dancing area. It's one thing to be a good dancer." She starts a seated Macarena. "It's another to be a good dance partner." Her eyes fix on Paolo.

He nearly chokes on his veggie-meat stuff. "No, Mom. Please, no."

Mom stands and holds her hand out to Paolo. He looks like she's holding an ice pick to his eyeball.

Her voice drops. "Up. Now."

Paolo slumps for a second, then he stands and takes her hand.

28

She hums out. "If it hadn't been for Cotton-Eyed Joe . . ."

I'm stunned into paralysis by a rehash of the terror I endured earlier. Mom is enthusiastically clodhopping around the kitchen. She makes all the same moves as the dancers in the videos, but she's a coffeed-up version. My brother is the zombie version. Every couple of turns he glares over at me. I'm in for an epic wedgie for bringing this up. Finally, after nearly knocking over a chair, Mom makes a little bow.

"Thank you, kind sir," she says.

Paolo sits down and starts shoveling glop in his mouth before she can go for round two.

"Mom, I really, really, really do not want to dance. Whose idea was it anyway to put dancing in P.E.?" I say.

"I had to do it when I was your age too. I don't know, Lupe. It's just always been around." Mom lays her hand on my cheek. "There are battles worth fighting. Like the dress code thing or your bubbles." She gives my cheek a quick pinch. "Those, my dear, are good causes. But getting rid of a few weeks of dancing, that isn't one of them." She spoons stew onto my plate. "Learn to dance." She cocks her head to one side and makes stiff robot moves with her arms and legs. "See? It's freeing."

She can't possibly understand. Dancing is her superpower to embarrass me. Even though she knows my deal with Uncle Hector and how badly I need this A, it doesn't look like I'll get any support from her. So when we finish eating, I slink away while she's busy doing some dance she calls the running man.

I need Andy.

29

I hurry to take a shower. (Not because of Paolo's stupid prayer.) I wash up and shave the two hairs on my right armpit.

I sit down at the one and only computer in the house, where everyone knows all your business. I click on Andy's number and the computer chirps. Andy's face pops up. She has a big white glob of toothpaste on her forehead, but the zit underneath pokes through the center like a cherry on top of whipped cream.

"Can I come over?" I ask.

"What about *Doctor Who*?"

I shrug. "Niles can't tonight for some reason."

Andy flinches back. "Weird."

I'm glad it's not just me. "Anyway, can I come over?"

Andy smiles. "I bet I know what this is about." Her mom's a door-crack listener, so Andy is half whispering. "My mom did her usual . . ." Andy makes her signature hand puppet. "'How was your day, dear? What did you learn? Did you eat all your lunch?'" She puts her hand down. "Anyway, I told her about square dancing . . ."

"Let me guess," I say. "She started dancing."

Andy's eyes widen. "If you can call it that. She started kicking her legs out from side to side."

I imagine her mom in their perfect museum of a house, wearing her high heels on their marble floors, flapping around like a flamingo on ice.

"And, Lupe . . ." Andy shuts her eyes so tight they look like they might suck into her brain.

"What is it?" I ask.

30

"My mom yelled, 'Grab your partner!' and arm-locked me into a twirl."

I slap my hand over my mouth.

"Apparently it's an official thing," she says. "It's universal. They all did it."

"I know. My mom told me. There should be a warning label on it or something. Do they even know how awful this is?" I ask.

"Do you think they're brainwashed with subliminal messages by the guy calling out the dance moves?" Andy crinkles her forehead and a flake of toothpaste falls off.

"That's one theory," I say. "There has to be a way to stop this."

"How'd it go with Coach Solden after school?"

I give her the thumbs-down. "Can I borrow your laptop when I come over?"

"I guess. We can tell my mom you're writing a letter to the producers to complain about how long it is between *Doctor Who* seasons."

I'm about to object. Instead, I grab a Post-it note and a pen. I jot down out of Andy's line of sight, *Protest letter to BBC.*

"What do you really need the laptop for?" she asks.

I motion with my eyes toward the kitchen. "I want to do some research without an audience." The smell of soaking cornhusks drifts into my room.

Abuela Salgado's voice blares over speakerphone. "¡Le vas a poner pasas a los tamales! ¿Sí o no?"

Andy jumps. "Why's your grandma so mad?"

"She's not mad. She just has strong opinions on things. My

31

mom refuses to put raisins in her tamales." I agree with Mom. But I'm not ready to make weird food segregation one of my causes.

"Hmmm. Imagine that," Andy says. "Your grandma has strong opinions."

"Very funny," I say. She doesn't even know how Grandma Wong feels about putting cilantro in ha gao. Genetically speaking, I didn't stand a chance.

Mom hangs up, and within a few seconds Missy Elliott starts rapping her own strong opinions from my mom's phone.

Andy shrugs. "Your mom's still way less embarrassing than mine. At least *your* mom doesn't make you listen to Enya."

Andy doesn't know it, but behind her face on the monitor, my mom is squirming around like she's having contractions.

CHAPTER 4

Mrs. Washington greets me at the door of Andy's house wearing her usual pencil skirt and fancy blouse. "¡Hola, Guadalupe!" she says way too loudly. "Ni hao!"

I bite back a smile. I'm not sure why Mrs. Washington thinks yelling is necessary, but it's an improvement from when she used to call out, "Feliz cumpleaños," then a "Wo ai ni" follow-up. I think it's her way of trying to understand my cultures after my failed Mexinese ethnicity-bubble campaign.

"Ni hao, Mrs. Washington," I say back.

A full nasal assault of a vanilla Glade PlugIns greets me as I walk in. I slip off my flip-flops. My feet hit the cold marble and a shiver runs from my toes up my legs.

Andy's mom has replaced their couch pillows . . . again, and yet another new "Live, Laugh, Love" sign hangs over the fireplace.

Our mantel still has decades of smoke stains and dried orange petals left over from Día de los Muertos. I'm pretty sure Andy's mom single-handedly keeps HomeGoods in business.

"Andalusia tells me you two are working on something this evening," she says.

"Uh, yeah, something," I answer.

"Could it possibly have anything to do with . . ." She smiles and skips backward a few steps, which is an interesting move, but I don't think has anything to do with square dancing.

I avert my eyes hoping she won't snag my arm into a twirl. "Yep."

She re-tucks her blouse into her waistband. "I know it's not your thing, Guadalupe," she says, giving me a quick hug. "Someday you might look back on this as something you actually enjoyed." She gives a wince and holds her lower back after that move. "Ooph . . . enjoy your youth."

I snort. "No offense. But, I don't have time to enjoy my youth."

Mrs. Washington presses her lips together, then a laugh escapes. "Well, I have faith that you and Andy are going to find a way."

"Thanks for believing in us, I guess," I say, shrugging.

She hands me a bowl of carrots, celery, and hummus off the coffee table. "Take this up with you, will you?"

"Yum," I say flatly.

"And don't forget to chew properly." She smiles and taps my shoulder. "You don't have to do the recommended thirty-two, but I find a good dozen chews is perfect."

I guess I should be glad that Mrs. Washington cares about me enough to hope I'm both happy and have good digestion.

"Andalusia!" Mrs. Washington yells out. I know Andy is somewhere rolling her eyes at her full name.

Her voice echoes down. "In my room."

I run upstairs, hoping someday I'll live in a house where I get to walk up actual stairs to my room.

When I get there, Andy's dad is standing in her doorway. "Hey kid," he says, hitting the bill of my hat and turning to leave. He's dressed in some sort of Lycra running suit I think is meant to turn his sweat into natural energy. "You two behave." He gives Andy a mock-serious look, then grins at us and disappears downstairs.

I flop onto Andy's bed. Her new soft, cream comforter is like an alpaca and a Snuggie had a baby. My bed still has the *Barbie: Mermaidia* comforter I insisted on in the first grade. I've flipped it over to the bubble side, but Andy still knows what horror lurks on the other side.

Andy's closet door is open. The closet is almost as big as my entire room. On one half her jeans and T-shirts hang unfaded and wrinkle-free. Shoes are sorted neatly into cubbies and shiny necklaces she's never worn are hanging from a jewelry organizer.

But the other side of the closet is magical. Undissected owl-puke balls sit in a shoebox on one half of a long table. Tiny bones she's extracted from the owl pellets are carefully placed in piles next to an X-Acto knife.

The rest of the desk is a miniature model of a mouse city. A

35

gold and red "Welcome to New Yack!" sign is set in swirly letters like it's an English village. We had a few ideas like Barfsberg, Chunksylvania, and so on, but we settled on New Yack because it sounded classy. Even a pub called The Boney Rodent has two mouse skeletons sitting at the bar holding tiny mugs.

Besides the twelve-year-old English girl who creates sonatas and concertos, the kid from Memphis who fused an atom, or the Indian boy who created the smallest operational satellite, it's about the most impressive thing I've seen a kid our age do. It's cool she lets me help pick out names and build stuff every once in a while. But I act casual about it so I don't get sucked too far into Andy's mousehole. I'm pretty sure this isn't what Mrs. Washington hoped and dreamed Andy would create when Andy asked to go to the dollhouse aisle at the craft store. But Mrs. Washington lets Andy keep it hidden behind closed closet doors, "as long as she keeps the rest of her life in order."

Cobbled streets and lanterns surround the field mouse grave-yard that's lined with tiny headstones, all with the same last name of Rodentia. My favorite, Paco Rodentia, was mysteriously missing a leg when Andy chiseled him from the barf clump, so she glued a fake leg on him. Somewhere in mouse heaven, Paco's hobbling around on a prosthetic toothpick.

Andy grabs her laptop from the shelf above The Boney Rodent and closes the closet door. We sit on her bed and put the computer on a pillow in front of us. Andy slides it closer to me so I can start my research.

"Can I ask you something?" she asks.

"Sure."

"Why is this so important to you? I mean, can't you just let this square dancing thing go?"

I love Andy and she's usually pretty sensitive to this stuff, but she just can't know what it's like to never be able to see your dad again. She wouldn't understand how it feels, knowing that the last thing he told me was to never give up on things I believe in.

"No," I answer. "I can't let it go."

"I wish my mom understood that I had my own ideas." Andy's picking at her thumbnail, which means she's nervous to tell me something. "Now my mom wants me to play club soccer on top of everything else."

I actually jump back. "Club soccer!" We both know the club soccer girls at school only hang out together. No outsiders. "You can't!"

"It was that or ballet! She thinks it's the perfect next step toward becoming a well-rounded model citizen." Andy sighs. "Apparently I need to do some sort of group activity on top of everything else."

I guess I should cut her some slack. "But ballet or soccer?" I say. "That means you have to choose Samantha or Jordyn?"

Jordyn is the Samantha of club soccer. She leads. The others follow.

"Who would you pick?" Andy asks.

She's right. At least Jordyn won't humiliate her on a daily basis.

"You don't know how lucky you are," she says. "Your mom is

37

happy no matter what you do." Andy picks at her thumbnail again. "I just want my mom and dad to be proud of me."

I try to imagine my mom making Paolo or me do something we hated. "You'll be a good soccer player, Andy."

Andy stops picking at her nail and looks up. "Thanks," she says, smiling.

We sit back and find "Cotton-Eyed Joe" on YouTube. Way more than I expect pops up. The song made some big comeback as a line dance. I can't let my mom find out that tidbit.

We skip past the learn-to-dance videos and find a bunch about the history of square dancing. I scroll down: "The History of Square Dancing—Ozark Rag," "The History of Square Dancing—Virginia Reel," "The History of Square Dancing—Cotton-Eyed Joe."

Bingo! "Cotton-Eyed Joe" is a good five minutes longer than any of the others. I must be able to find some valuable ammo in there. I hit play.

A man wearing overalls and a straw hat grins back at us. "Welcome back to *Billy Bob's Southern Square Dance Nation*." A little stalk of wheat seesaws in his mouth as he talks. I get that square dancing is supposed to be an *American* tradition, but I'm as American as anyone else, and there's nothing about this guy that I relate to at all. "Tonight we're chewing the fat on the old time favorite, 'Cotton-Eyed Joe.' 'Cotton-Eyed Joe' predates the Civil War. It was sung by slaves on Southern plantations, and is thought to refer to a man making his rounds with the ladies."

I glance at Andy and she shrugs.

"American history is pretty messed up," I say.

She nods but doesn't say anything. I know sometimes there's a lot more in what people don't say out loud.

The man winks and continues. "But why are his eyes white as cotton?" The farmer guy's eyebrows rise so high they disappear under the brim of his hat. "Could be glaucoma? Or maybe cataracts?" He raises his arms above his head in question. "But if one listens carefully to the words, poor ol' Cotton-Eyed Joe's eyes were whited over by chlamydia or syphilis—"

I hit pause. "Do you know what any of those words mean?"

"I don't know," Andy says. "Greek goddesses?"

I open another window and start typing in Google: *K-L-A-M-I-* Chlamydia pops up as a suggestion just below. My hands go a little clammy. The word looks way more grown-up and serious than something we should be looking at.

Andy's mom might be strict, but because of her whole "well-rounded kids" thing, she doesn't believe in filters. I take a breath and hover over *chlamydia* and hit enter. Within a few seconds I'm finding more out about the guy Joe than I should know.

Chlamydia: a widespread, often asymptomatic sexually transmitted disease caused by Chlamydia trachomatis.

I type in *S-I-F-I. Syphilis* pops up this time. I hit enter.

Syphilis: a sexually transmitted disease caused by the spirochete bacterium Treponema pallidum.

Andy gasps.

39

I go back to the YouTube video and hit play.

"That's right. Cotton-Eyed Joe was doing a little more than farming, folks—"

I hit pause again.

Andy and I turn to each other, eyes wide and mouths open. I fall to the ground and giggle, rolling into a ball like an armadillo. "Oh, man. This is too good."

But Andy's not moving. She stares straight ahead stiffly like she just walked in on her parents making out. "I don't even know what all this means."

We can't be the only ones who've noticed all this before. "It means we just won, Andy. We don't even take sex ed. until the end of next quarter." I sit back on the bed. "We can put a stop to square dancing now."

I close out YouTube and open PowerPoint. I click on the first slide and type . . .

Square Dancing is Directly Related to Sex and Corruption of Youth!

CHAPTER 5

One of the first articles to pop up on a Cotton-Eyed Joe Google search shows he could've also gotten his cloudy eyes from alcohol poisoning. It's Andy's idea to make all the words swirl or ripple into the screen to hint at something wobbly and disorienting.

"Are you sure this is going to work?" Andy says.

"If the disease thing doesn't work, we can amp up the moonshine angle. Grown-ups don't want us to see that stuff yet."

"We're going to cover human sexuality and controlled substances next quarter anyway," she says.

"That's the thing. They *have* to educate us about it. But they don't want us actually . . ." I wink. ". . . *thiiiinnnnking* about it, if you get my meaning."

Andy's mouth and nose skew to one side. I don't think she gets it.

"Maybe instead we should just bring up the point that square dancing is an outdated tradition and has nothing to do with Americans in recent history?" she says. "I mean, what does it have to do with us? Why is square dancing any more important than Kabuki, or Bollywood, or break dancing?"

She's right. The whole thing feels wrong. But none of that will matter if I can make it stop immediately. And the most direct path is to shock the heck out of them. "I agree with you. But we don't want them to get distracted by a side topic."

Andy falls back into her pillow with a sigh. I can't tell if she's just tired or annoyed with me, but I'm nearly done and out of her hair.

I open the last PowerPoint slide and type my grand finale statement in all caps.

"Done." I hit save.

I log on to my student portal on the school website.

I find Principal Singh's email address and hit compose. I type Coach Solden's after CC. I can't help snickering. "Coach is gonna eat her words. 'You'll make a marvelous do-si-do-er,'" I mimic under my breath.

Good evening, Principal Singh.

I would like to request an emergency meeting during lunch tomorrow. I know Coach Solden will want to be there also. I have something very interesting and informative you'd both like to see.

Our school's reputation is at stake.

Andy interrupts right before I hit send. "You aren't going to attach the PowerPoint?"

"No way. I want to see their faces in real time."

Andy's voice is shifting. She's definitely had enough. "And how exactly are you going to show it to them without my computer?"

My stomach flips. I'm used to handling my causes on my own, so I sort of forgot it was her computer. But I was kind of hoping Andy would be there with me to gasp and cover her eyes for emphasis. "You aren't coming too?"

"You know I have jazz band practice Tuesday during lunch," she says.

I clasp my hands together, droop my face, and make sad eyes.

She throws up her hands. "Just keep it in the sleeve."

I pat her shoulder. "I owe you."

I continue typing. I am happy to meet you in your office during the lunch period. I sign, Andy and Lupe.

Andy props herself up on her elbows. "Wait. Why are you putting my name too? I just said I can't be there."

"They'll be more likely to let me talk if they think I'm not acting alone," I say. "Pleeeeaase."

"Fine." She falls back into the pillow again, this time with her hands balled into fists.

I hit send before she changes her mind.

***

Principal Singh opens her door the next day during lunch. She's holding a cup of coffee and wearing what my mom calls a "serious suit." Steam spirals up ominously to her face, making her look even more stern. Coach Solden is there too, sitting on the other side of the desk, holding her own coffee.

"Good afternoon, Lupe." Coach Solden leans over, trying to look out the door behind me. "Where's Andy?"

"Uh, something came up."

"It did, did it?" She sets her cup down and crosses her arms over her chest. "I can't wait to see what's so important that Principal Singh and I missed our lunchtime Zumba for educators."

I ignore the TacoTime wrappers crumpled on the desk and try not to imagine the two of them, or any other sweaty teachers, doing the cha-cha to an "Ice Ice Baby" remix.

"I promise this won't take much time, but it *will* be worth it." I pull Andy's laptop out of my backpack.

Principal Singh sits at her desk. Should I ask her if she'll move next to Coach for the show? I don't want to push my luck. I open the laptop at the end of the desk. The screen glows. My PowerPoint is already queued up.

"I was under the impression you wanted to *talk* with us about something." Principal Singh motions to the computer. "If this is some sort of video, you could have just sent it."

I keep my chin high and posture straight. "What I have to show you here, you should see together . . . for support."

44

They make brief eye contact and both quickly take a sip of coffee.

If speech class taught me one thing, it's how to get an emotional response. Visual props for emphasis are best. Evoking a gag reflex to square dancing will definitely get it banned.

I hit the space bar. The whited-over eyeball I found pops up. But this isn't a plain ol' "cotton-eye." Bonus crusts coat the eyelashes. A green mucous glob drips down one corner, with a maggot crawling down the other.

Only downfall, I found the eye on a guy with half his face missing too, so I'm pretty sure the original helpful graphic wasn't real. But this cropped, magged-up version does the trick.

Principal Singh spits her coffee back into her cup. Her entire body lurches forward. "Oh, gawd," she barely gets out.

We have gag, check!

"Yep," I say. "Square dancing."

"Wait a minute." Coach Solden leans toward the computer and squints. "Is that from *Zombie Apocalypse II*?"

I reach over as fast as I can and hit the space bar. "Moving on."

Slide two pops up. It's an image of a Petri dish filled with what looks like hairy, green Jell-O.

Principal Singh wipes coffee spray off her desk. "I'm assuming there's a point to all this. I'm hoping you didn't just call this meeting in an attempt to make us sick."

"Of course not." I hit the space bar again. *Chlamydia trachomatis* pops up under the greenish-grey fuzz. I hit the space bar again. *The cause of Joe's "cotton-eye."* "I was as surprised as you are. I just happened upon an interesting documentary of sorts."

Coach Solden takes a deep breath and closes her eyes. Principal Singh is covering her mouth.

I lean in for effect. "It turns out Cotton-Eyed Joe likely had a disease caused by *you-know-what*."

Now, they're both staring at me. I can't get a read on either of them. The silence is getting awkward so I hit the space bar again. The farmer guy's Southern accent from the YouTube video twangs out, "That's right. Cotton-Eyed Joe was doing a little more than farming, folks."

I widen my eyes and shake my head in mock disappointment.

This was supposed to be my pausing place for emphasis. By this point they should both be scrambling to apologize for the years of torture and corruption they'd exposed kids to. But they're both sitting completely straight-faced.

I have no choice.

I hit the space bar for the next slide. It's an image of a guy slumped over in a jail cell, holding a bottle of whiskey. I've Photoshopped one of his eyes to be white. I've added in "Joe—Life Sentence for Corrupting our Youth" above the jail cell.

I cringe and try to make a little gasp, but it comes out more like a hiccaburp. I really wish I had Andy here to scream.

Principal Singh hasn't budged and Coach Solden is now slowly sipping her coffee.

46

I've got to wrap this thing up with a bang. I hit the keyboard. My final statement pops up.

IF ISSAQUAH MIDDLE SCHOOL ALLOWS "COTTON-EYED JOE" INTO THE CURRICULUM . . . THE ENTIRE SEVENTH GRADE CLASS WILL END UP IN JUVIE!

"So, Coach Solden, Principal Singh." I narrow my eyes for emphasis. I take time to make eye contact with each of them like we were taught. And I make my voice raspy like the salt-and-pepper-haired guy on the *Dateline Mystery* show. "With every 'Where did you come from Cotton-Eyed Joe,' we are reminded of sex, drugs, and . . . square dancing." I reach over and grab the top edge of the computer. "Juuuvieeeee . . ." I finish, closing the laptop at the same time.

Coach Solden rolls her eyes (must be shock) and Principal Singh turns in her seat and bows her head (horror and shame).

"Well Lupe, that was quite a slide show." Principal Singh folds one hand over the other on her desk. "I'm not sure where you are getting your correlations, but I appreciate your concern and effort. I will take all that I've heard under advisement and do what's best for the students."

The bell rings and Coach Solden picks up her coffee and clip-board. She flicks her hand at me in a shooing motion. I take this as approval. I see the hint of what looks like a smile on her face.

I walk out and promptly put my ear to the closed door.

"Wow," Principal Singh says. "Can you believe that?" It's muffled, but the words are clear enough. My heart is pounding, and I feel like jumping, but they might hear me.

That can only mean my presentation was a success. Just as I'm making a victorious fist pump, the school janitor, Mr. Helms, pushes his broom around the corner. He shakes his head and continues on.

I can barely focus on where I'm going. "Wrong period, Lupe," Mr. Lundgren says from his desk when I walk into science class.

I turn around and continue toward the gym. I've finally won. I'll forever be known as the kid who ended square dancing. No one will ever make fun of me or my causes again. But most importantly, P.E. will go back to normal. I'll get straight As and I'll meet Fu Li Hernandez. Dad would definitely approve.

I don't need to tell everyone what I've done for them. They'll know it was me anyway.

I walk into the locker room and hand Andy her laptop.

"Thanks," I whisper. "I owe you one."

"How'd it go?"

I can only smile back.

She grabs my hands. "You did it?" she asks too loudly.

We back away from each other quickly. We need to remain calm. We'd agreed not to tell anyone just yet if I was successful, so we didn't jinx it.

"Looks that way," I say out of the side of my mouth, getting

48

my stuff ready for class. "Now we can get back to basketball and volleyball like normal kids."

Samantha and Claire are tying their hair up in buns and securing them with pencils. "This whole square dancing thing is stupid," Samantha says. There's one thing she and I actually agree on. "I mean, I take *professional* dancing." She lifts up on her toes for a split second. Even in her gym clothes, she looks like a swan. "*This* is a waste of time."

"My dad says it's part of the American way of life," another Pencil Bun says. "It would take a miracle or a genius to get us out of it."

Before I can stop myself, I blurt out loud enough for Samantha to overhear. "My presentation had Principal Singh so freaked out, I wouldn't be surprised if they outlawed square dancing in the entire school district."

"Lupe!" Andy shakes her head in warning. "Don't . . ."

One side of Samantha's mouth curls up like the Grinch. "Hey Claire. Lupe here says she got them to outlaw square dancing."

They all start laughing.

"Whatever," I say. "You'll thank me later."

Andy pulls me out of the locker room and into the gym. "Why'd you do that?"

I slump a little. "I don't know. I couldn't help myself."

Niles is already out and runs across the court to join us. Coach Solden blows her whistle. Within thirty seconds the rest of the boys and girls have piled out of the locker rooms.

"Sorry I was delayed. I had an important meeting," she says, tipping her head at me. "I have a special announcement."

49

Andy nudges my arm. I nudge her back. This is it.

Coach claps her hands in three loud pops. "Someone . . ." She glances at me. ". . . brought to the attention of Principal Singh that the square dancing song we were using might be inappropriate."

Samantha's mouth drops open. "No way . . ."

Coach Solden continues, "All P.E. classes will no longer be dancing to 'Cotton-Eyed Joe.'"

For a second there is complete silence.

Gordon Schnelly is the first to react. "But I practiced with my grandma." The gap-toothed smile he's had on during this entire square-dancing debacle falls.

"You did it?" Niles whispers.

Clapping begins to echo in the gym, and gets louder and louder. Two boys high-five and start dancing around—to celebrate not having to dance. A girl I've never heard speak before makes an awkward whoop that sounds like she has a bubble lodged in her throat. Everyone except Gordon has huge smiles on their faces. Even Samantha and Claire are staring at me in amazement.

Now's the time. I give Blake our baseball signal for a sacrifice bunt, and he grins in acknowledgement. I'm going to be legendary.

Mumbles go around the gym along with the clapping. In the fastest game of telephone ever, all forty kids know I was behind the change in a matter of seconds.

Niles pats me on the shoulder.

I suck in my gut and stand taller.

Coach Solden screeches her whistle four sharp times,

50

bringing the gym to an echoed silence. She's looking right at me. The same hint of a smile she had on her face earlier after our meeting is back. She winks at me and hits play on her stereo. It sounds like the ice cream truck has pulled up outside. She yells over the familiar music.

"This means everything you learned yesterday goes out the window. We start over. We'll now be twirling our partners to 'Turkey in the Straw'!"

Pinpricks run over my face and scalp, then down my back all the way to my butt.

Blake's arms are now firmly at his sides and he's giving me an annoyed look.

The semicircle of girls with messy buns surrounding Samantha is glaring at me. I half expect the pencils to catapult out of their buns in my direction. I turn to Andy. She's biting her lower lip and her face looks like a puppy's caught chewing on a slipper.

My own face turns hot and my ears are ringing, but I clearly hear Gordon yell out, "Yee-haw!"

Coach Solden skips around the table pretending it's her dance partner. She balances her CD player on her shoulder. Fiddles echo throughout the gym, then . . .

Turkey in the hay, in the hay, in the hay.
Turkey in the straw, in the straw, in the straw,
Pick up your fiddle and rosin your bow,
And put on a tune called Turkey in the Straw.

51

I'm in even worse shape than before. There's nothing disgusting in those lyrics I could even begin to argue against.

A quick image of Fu Li Hernandez holding his hand up for a high five just like Dad flashes in my mind. I hardly ever cry. Not even when I broke my big toe on Paolo's weight set. But right now, I want to.

How am I ever going to meet Fu Li if I have to learn to dance better than girls like Samantha? All my hard work was for nothing.

I rack my brain for a solution, but it's pretty clear there's only one way I have a chance.

CHAPTER 6

If I'm doing this, it'll be on my own terms. So, an hour and a half after school ends, I'm kicking my pillow out of the way to make a bigger dance area on my bedroom floor. I bow to Andy; she bows back.

"And . . . go." I start with a sideways step.

"Ouch!"

I yank my foot off Andy's. "Sorry."

Andy puts her hand on my shoulder. A tiny piece of what looks like grey fur hangs off one of her dark curls. I reach out and flick it onto the ground, hoping it's not from one of her owl pellets.

"Do you want me to lead instead?" she asks with sympathetic eyes.

"No. I'm gonna get this. If we practice together every day and make sure we end up as partners, we can make top eight in the class and get the A we need."

"You mean, the A *you* need," she says.

"I know, I know," I say. "I'm gonna owe you big time."

She casually boops me on the nose. Our own secret hand-shake seemed clever when we were six. Now, it's starting to seem unsanitary. "It all evens out in the end," she says. "Remember when I peed my pants in the fourth grade?"

"Yeah." I shrug like it was no big deal, but it was one epic accident.

"My mom isn't the one who got Ms. Cox in trouble for not letting me go to the bathroom after I'd already asked four times." Her jaw is tight. "You did. You're the one who got equal potty rights for everyone even if we'd just been at recess. You're the one who made sure no one teased me." Andy's eyes are welling up a little.

I never actually told her I ruined my jacket too by throwing it over the pee puddle in her chair so no one would see.

"And that's just one of the times you've stood up for me." Andy makes a huge inhale through her nose and her nostrils flare. "We're a team, Lupe. We will get you that A."

I think she wants me to get the grade now as much as I do. I boop her nose and hold my hand out. "We're gonna get this."

After another five minutes of me stomping around on her toes, we decide to move into the living room, where we can at least put music on.

We sit at the desk for a quick break, Andy with a bag of

frozen peas on her feet. I pull up YouTube. There are even more videos of "Turkey in the Straw" than there were of "Cotton-Eyed Joe."

Little square pictures line the side of the monitor. A cartoon of a mutant, singing turkey leads the views on YouTube. But the same farmer-band I first watched playing "Cotton-Eyed Joe" has the next "Turkey in the Straw" video.

Even the Wiggles are on the list. Five men, each wearing a different color, stand in a row holding fiddles and banjos like five human Skittles at a hoedown.

"Seriously?" Andy moves closer to the screen like she can't believe her own eyes. "I used to love them."

I think we both feel betrayed. I click on the video.

They sway from one foot back to the other, arms folded in front of them like a metronome of synchronized ridiculousness. The video cuts to the purple Wiggle. He's traded in his purple shirt for a fluffy brown turkey suit. He's clucking around in front of a barn, a big smile on his face.

When I turn to Andy, her eyes are sagging. "They didn't seem this stupid when I was younger."

"That was when we were kids. We're pretty much mature adults now."

"True. Which video do we pick?" Andy says. "I can't focus with all that clucking and pecking around in the background."

There are others that look really old. It looks like some of them even have different words, but we need to stick to our P.E. class's version. "Let's just go with the one with the most views."

55

I rub my eyes, but the afterimage of the Wiggles remains. "I can't believe over 200,000 people have watched this." I hit play.

For some reason, having music doesn't make our dancing any better. Andy makes an overenthusiastic arm switch and punches me in the stomach. I get a little too confident on a spin and my forehead pummels into her shoulder. After another ten minutes or so, we take a break to let Andy ice her feet again. We decide we can learn faster if we find a video with someone calling out the instructions.

Almost all of the clips seem to be from the South or Midwest, and the couples look like they're straight out of some laundry-detergent TV ad from the fifties. I'm having a hard time figuring out why *this* dance is the one they're forcing us to do. None of the dancers even remotely look like me, or any of my grandparents for that matter.

We find the state square dancing convention of North Dakota. It looks more like a community center filled with seniors faced off in an elderly rumble. Andy hits play and the music starts. If those old fogeys can do this, I figure we can too. We do our best to keep up, but it turns out those geezers can really move.

The caller yells out over the fiddle. "The lady goes right. The gent goes left."

"Lupe! You're the gent!" Andy yells after our chests slam together yet again.

"I know." We face each other holding hands. "Wait, aren't we supposed to be side by side?"

After a few more minutes, we both have sweat dripping down our faces.

"Aces high, deuces low, promenade all the way you go. Little bit o' heel, little bit o' toe. Promenade and don't be slow."

A cackle from behind us drowns out the caller's next words. "Wow! Troglodytes really *can* dance." My brother is leaning against the doorjamb.

"Shut up, Paolo," I yell.

We try to ignore him, but now he's planted himself on the couch, one arm behind his head, the other cramming chicharrones in his mouth. Ironically, just like a troglodyte.

We nail a singular spin and we high-five. "We're going to have this down in no time. When Coach sees us dance together—"

"Ha! Good luck with that," Paolo mumbles through a full mouth.

"What's that supposed to mean?" I snap back. We continue promenading in perfect sync around the coffee table.

"It means, who said you two get to choose who you dance with?"

We turn in a half arc and promenade back the other way. "Why couldn't we?" Andy asks.

"Oh, this is too good. You really don't know?" He shoves another fistful of pork rinds into his mouth.

We stop in front of him and drop each other's hands. I turn off the music and glare at him in the silence. "Fine. Tell us then," I say.

"It's gonna cost you."

Andy wags her finger at him. "We aren't giving you anything."

Paolo licks chicharrón crumbs off his fingers one by one. "Then I guess you two can go back to wasting your time."

I grip Andy's arm. Paolo doesn't bluff. But he also drives a hard bargain.

"Fine, I do dishes tonight," I say with my opening bid.

"One week," he counters. "I unload. You load."

We both know loading is way worse. Chiseling cemented food out of the Crock-Pot is worse than using the PedEgg on Abuela Salgado's scaly bunions.

"I load, three days. Final offer," I say.

He smiles like he's weaseled me out of my entire year's allowance. "Deal."

"Okay then, tell us," I say.

He closes his eyes. But now, he doesn't look so smug. Paolo winces like he's reliving some awful nightmare.

"Not only do you have to say yes to whoever asks you . . ." Paolo opens his eyes and slowly looks each of us in the face. ". . . but square dancing at school is boy-ask-girl."

CHAPTER 7

"What did you say?"

"You two thought you were getting off that easy?" Paolo leans toward us. The entire world is suddenly in slow motion. "I said . . . You. Have. To. Dance. With. A. Boy." A cocky grin spreads over his face. "Ha!" He laughs so hard he snorts.

I try to move, but I can't. Someone just freeze-dried my brain. The idea that the school can force me to hold hands with a boy and spin around like a dented hula-hoop is so completely unfair, I'd scream except I don't want to give Paolo the satisfaction.

Andy grabs my arm and pulls me outside. Rain drizzle beads up on her hair as we just stare at each other.

"Coach never said anything about boys asking girls," I say. "Why doesn't anyone tell us about this stuff?"

"Yeah. It's like getting our boobs or periods. They keep it a secret, then, Whammo! Here's another life twist you just have to accept."

I nod like I understand, but I'm still pretty much flat as a tortilla. And the period thing . . . There's gotta be a way to stop *that* from happening. "What do we do now?" I say.

The rain that was a sprinkle a second ago is now coming down in glops.

Andy looks up at the clouds like they peed in her Cap'n Crunch. She pulls out her phone and types a text to her mom. "I gotta go. It's family cleaning night, and if I don't call dibs on the kitchen, I get stuck with my little brother's dribble on the bathroom floor."

She hits send. We sit in silence waiting. I think we're both in shock. Her mom eventually pulls up and rolls down the window.

"Hi, Mrs. Washington," I yell out over the rain.

"¡Buenas noches, Guadalupe!" she yells back.

"Vámonos, Andalusia," Mrs. Washington says. "Don't forget you have twenty minutes of piano, then thirty of coding practice before cleaning duty!"

Andy rolls her eyes. "See you tomorrow."

I boop her on the nose. She boops me back. This time I feel a sharp pain from what must be a sprouting stress zit inside my nose.

I walk back in the house. Thank God, Paolo's off the couch and the bathroom door is closed. I hear a flush from inside Azteca and I sprint to my room so I don't have to talk to him anymore.

60

I'm more tired after an hour of square dancing than I was after the timed 5K in P.E. Maybe this is what Coach was talking about: how some things that don't look like sports actually are. But, it's still dancing. And it's become exponentially worse now that I'm supposed to dance with a boy.

***

Coach Solden greets me cheerily the next day in her office. "Morning, Guadalupe. What can I do for you?"

"Just a quick question if you have time."

She takes a big swallow of coffee. "Shoot."

"So, Paolo said something, and I can't believe something so ridiculous could be true."

She nods. "Yep. I have a brother. What was it? Mine told me one in ten thousand births is from the anus instead of the uterus, and I was one of those butt babies."

My mouth drops and I'm pretty sure my eyes have expanded to three times their normal size.

She bites her lower lip and averts her eyes. "So . . . Nothing like that? Well, why don't you just tell me what Paolo told you?"

I plop down in the seat across from her. "Paolo says square dancing is boy-ask-girl."

"Yep," she says, like it's common knowledge.

A cherry bomb goes off in my stomach. "Why can't we just dance with a friend?"

"Like any sport, there are rules," she says. "This is one of them."

61

My brain immediately leaps to Niles. I gotta check with him what he decided with Mr. Lambert in LRC, but if he's going to dance, we could do it together. I don't think I've ever seen him dance, and he's definitely never seen *me* dance, but we're good enough athletes that we could probably make it work. There's no guarantee we would get that A, though.

And besides, that wouldn't solve the problem that the whole thing is just wrong on so many levels.

"Dumb rules should be changed, right?" My voice is cracking. I normally hold myself together better than this. "And this is definitely a dumb rule."

"Square dancing will teach you to work as a team with someone you might not have worked with before. Besides, it's been done this way—"

"I know, I know. Since 1938."

She sets her cup down. "Whether you like it or not, tomorrow each boy will ask a girl."

"Tomorrow?" I choke out.

"Yes, Lupe," she says. "We've already had a day's delay with the song change."

How did I screw this up so much? Can I tell Coach why it's so important? How I need to meet Fu Li and maybe figure out some stuff about my dad? If I say it out loud, it sounds too stupid.

I slump in the chair. *Don't cry. Don't cry.* I stare downward and force my chin to stop shaking.

"Can't Andy and I dance together? The caller says grab your

partner, not your boy partner, or girl partner." My eyes are starting to burn. "Please."

Coach's face softens, almost like she understands. She stares out the window. But she doesn't speak.

We sit in silence for forever, or maybe like ten seconds.

When she finally talks, she's quiet.

"Lupe. You can do this."

***

After school, I watch Niles kick our rock three times without me before he kicks it back. I'm sure it doesn't mean anything.

I'm still digesting everything Coach said.

I know I should just tell Niles what I found out about boys asking girls in front of the entire gym class. Except . . . I'm not sure it's my place. Maybe that's a Mr. Lambert and LRC thing. But, what if they just made sure Niles was okay with the dancing part and didn't warn him about the other stuff?

I jump in front of him to face him. "I need to talk to you."

"Okay," he says.

"Paolo told Andy and me that square dancing is going to be boy-ask-girl," I blurt out. "I verified it with Coach Solden today."

Niles's facial expression doesn't change.

"I should have told you earlier." Time to rip off the Band-Aid. "And there's more." I let out a breath. "Coach is making the boys ask the girls tomorrow."

He shrugs. "I know."

"What do you mean, you know?"

"I mean, I already talked about it with Mr. Lambert."

"And you're okay with it?"

"Well, I don't mind the dancing so much. It's not so different from learning my form in martial arts." He bends one elbow into his body and he swipes the other in front of him, one leg back. I see his point, but square dancing is nowhere as cool.

"It's my choice," he says. "And I'm in control of how I'll be touching people and who I ask. That's why I went to LRC to work it all out."

"Why didn't you tell me?" I ask.

"Sorry. I thought you knew."

I step back to the side of him and continue walking. "No." I sigh. "What a crappy day."

"Soooo, which part did you think was best?" he asks.

I think of my conversation with Coach and how the day never really improved. "It was all pretty bad."

He stops for a moment, his forehead crinkled. "I thought it was a great episode."

I realize we aren't talking about the same thing. "Do you mean *Doctor Who*?"

"Yeah, we haven't had a chance to catch up yet." He continues walking, and I have to admit I'm grateful to think about something else for a minute.

"Oh, well," I say. "I liked how when the rotting meatball

creatures were about to be obliterated by the Furwimpians, they morphed into one giant meatball."

He nods. "Yeah, that was pretty cool."

"What about you?" I ask.

He doesn't answer immediately. "Well, I liked how the Doctor took time to understand them and what they were trying to say. Even with their differences and when things got chaotic, he waited until things calmed down and found a way to listen and understand them."

"I get that," I say.

When we get to my gate, Niles picks up our rock. "See ya in the morning."

"Bye, Furwimpian."

"Bye, rotting meatball," he says, waving over his head.

Next door, Delia is filling birdseed into a feeder that's swaying from a metal garden hook. The Nuñez's cat is sitting directly under the falling seed, looking up expectantly.

"What do you think, Fletcher?" she says to the cat. "Won't this make for beautiful bird-watching?"

I'm almost positive I see Fletcher lick his lips in response.

"Hey Delia," I call out.

She turns toward me and a dusting of birdseed from the feeder embeds in her hair. "Good afternoon, Lupe. Anything thought-provoking happen at school?"

I think of the boys I'm going to be spinning around with. "The opposite of thought-provoking."

She tilts her head in concern. "Anything you care to discuss?"

I consider for a moment the conversation we'd have. Every last ounce of Delia's psychology can't help me process this. I sigh. "No thanks. Maybe tomorrow."

"Well, you know where to find me if you change your mind," she says.

I drag my feet into the house and to my room. I drop my backpack and flop onto my bed. I stare at the ceiling. The shadows begin to shift as it gets darker outside. By the time I hear my mom's car rattle into the driveway, I've still come up with nothing to help my situation. The front door squeaks open a minute later, followed by her footsteps.

Mom comes in and sits on the edge of my bed. "Becky Solden called me."

"Again? Do teachers have an app, so you can tell each other what your own kids did during the day?" I cover my face with my pillow. "If I have to dance, it shouldn't have to be with a boy."

"I'm not saying I disagree with you," she replies. I can tell by the tone of her voice, she sorta does agree with me. "But it's not going to kill you to dance with a boy. You play sports with these same boys all the time."

"That's different," I say.

What she doesn't know is that by now even my teammates have heard about the song change and probably think I'm a loser. But that's not the important thing. I should be able to choose who I have to twirl around with in front of everyone. If we don't have a choice, we shouldn't have to dance at all.

"I mean, what if I'm gay?" I ask. "Shouldn't I be able to dance with a girl?"

"Are you gay?"

"I don't know. I'm only twelve. I thought I'd figure it out in a few years."

She pulls the pillow off my face and rubs my head. "So, is this about not wanting to square dance, or not wanting to dance with boys?"

"Both." I am suddenly missing my dad. I try to pull the pillow back over my head but she stops me. "Everything," I say. "My life's a disaster. I'm probably going to get a boob or two any day now, and I have a zit ready to explode inside my nostril. Do they have to make middle school worse with square dancing?"

Behind Mom, Fu Li's rookie card hangs on my wall. I know Fu Li isn't Dad or anything. But his smile sparkles just like Dad's when he still played ball.

Fu Li didn't quit to go work on some fishing boat, though. My dad did. And that's not going to be me.

I'm afraid to tell my mom about why I need to meet Fu Li so badly. She's done so much to make sure Paolo and I are okay. I'd never want her to think she wasn't enough.

I wonder for a moment what my dad would say about all this.

"I miss Dad." My voice cracks a little. "A lot."

67

"Me too," she answers quietly. "Every day." It's silent for a moment before she continues. "But you know he's always with us."

I look right into her eyes. So far her feelings don't seem hurt. I take a deep breath. "Mom?"

"Yes?" She leans in smiling.

I'm still nervous to come right out and say it. "There's something I can't explain."

"Try," Mom says.

"Something about Dad . . . and Fu Li." My stomach pretzels. "Meeting him is not just about baseball." There's no way I can say out loud that I need to meet someone who didn't compromise on their dream, without sounding like I'm beating up on my dad.

My mom tilts her head. "I'm not sure I understand."

"I just need to meet Fu Li. I think it will help me with some other stuff about Dad."

My mom hugs me, and when she sits back up, her eyes are watery. "Then make it happen," she says.

I sit up quickly, knocking the pillow to the ground. "Then you agree with me?"

She takes a deep breath. "Understanding how someone feels and agreeing with them aren't the same. I know you work hard to get As in all your classes. I just think you might be going about this the wrong way." She pats my head. "You know, dancing is good for the soul." She's up now and doing some sort of ripply belly dance. She slowly returns to normal human mode and lays her hand on my head. "Figure out another way to get your A in P.E. so you can meet Fu Li."

This talk was good even though it didn't go exactly how I expected. I'm glad I can talk to Mom about Fu Li. But why is it so hard to find a single adult who understands how damaging square dancing is, and who'd be on my side?

Then it hits me. Delia. How could I have not put it together? With her clout as a child psychologist, she single-handedly got the school start time changed from 7:25 to 8:10. For that alone, she's one of my favorite grown-ups anyway.

There's got to be some study out there about boys asking girls to dance, and the damage it causes to the girl having to say yes. And I'm sure it's detrimental in some way to the boy too, but that's not my problem right now. All I need is Delia on my side.

I take my mom's hand from my head and squeeze it. "Mom, do we have enough food for a guest tonight?"

***

Mom spoons tonight's reddish-brown goop out of the Crock-Pot into our bowls.

"So, I was thinking," I say.

Mom and Delia exchange a quick glance.

Paolo is busy separating what looks like shriveled ketchup-coated peas off to one side in his bowl.

"Yeeeeessss?" Delia leans in like she's about to analyze something important. She pulls her reading glasses from the top of her head onto her nose and her hair fans out to double its size. Her eyes magnify to double their size too.

69

"There's this whole square dancing thing going on at school right now," I say. I turn a little in my seat and face Delia, pretending not to see the look Mom gives me.

"I *loved* square dancing." Delia claps her hands together.

Not what I was hoping for.

This might not go as easily as I thought. I clear my throat. "I'm not saying some people don't like it and all, but don't you think it might be harmful?" I ask.

My mom sighs deeply, but Delia puts her elbow right on top of her silverware. "Harmful, Lupe? In what way?"

And . . . I'm in! "What if it damages our brains . . ."

My mom snorts. But when I look back at Delia, she's furrowing her brow. I've got her mulling it over. I've got to strike now while she's in doctor-duty mode.

". . . and . . . and self-esteem by dancing with a partner against our will?" I continue. "We could be permanently scarred."

Delia's forehead smoothes out again. "You'll be fine." She picks up her spoon and stirs her sludge.

Well, that took even less than our normal thirty seconds.

I prop one elbow onto the table and rest my chin in my hand. I shovel in a bite of tomato-pasta goop. I shouldn't have put Andy's toothpaste zit-remedy inside my nose before dinner. Now it tastes like there's mint mixed with tomato sauce in my mouth.

Mom wipes red stuff from the side of her lip. "Lupe. I still don't understand why you're making such a big deal of this. If anything, I've taught you to take the bull by the horns. Just ask a boy you don't mind dancing with so much."

70

My voice squeaks. "Girls can't ask boys."

Delia's head wrinkle is back. "What? Well, that's a bit archaic."

Mom sets her fork down. "You didn't tell me that part. I thought you just didn't want to dance with a boy."

Anddddd . . . I'm back in! "I don't. But I definitely shouldn't have to dance with some random boy who asks me."

"Are the boys really that bad?" Delia says, tilting her head. "Or are you using that as an excuse?"

I flick my wrist like I've seen adults do when they don't want to dwell on something. "Not the point. If a system is flawed, they should scrap it."

"I don't see them eliminating square dancing all together. It's been around for too long. But if you feel this strongly that it needs modification, you could always start a petition on Change.org."

Delia tends to take things to the extreme. I'm pretty sure Change.org is for stuff like protecting people from rogue governments, or saving lives.

Mom turns to Paolo. "You never told me you asked a girl." She reaches over and pinches his cheek. "How Rico Suave of you! Who was it?"

Paolo looks like he got caught on the toilet with half a sheet left. His head drops forward and he stares down, suddenly very focused on his plate.

"Yeah, Paolo." I think of the dishes I have to do after dinner because of our deal. "Who waaaaaas it?"

Mom ruffles his hair. "You have to tell us all the details."

Delia taps her fork on her bowl, like it's a pen on paper. "Yes. I'm curious how the experience made you feel, Paolo."

Paolo swallows and coughs. He makes way too big of a deal waving us off like he's got a noodle lodged in his esophagus. He jumps up from the table and runs to the bathroom.

I can tell a stall when I see one. His was good, though, and I know he's not coming back to the inquisitors.

"Guadalupe." Delia holds a finger in the air.

This is it! What I've been hoping for. Delia's come up with something I can use.

"Why not ask a boy in private? A friend," she says. "Make an arrangement with him so he knows when he asks, that you'll say yes? That way you are both comfortable with the situation."

The excitement I felt a second ago vanishes. Delia doesn't exactly know my current reputation. On top of that, it's too late. Tomorrow is the day. Plus, the only boy at school who even talks to me—

Mom and Delia stare at me as I scarf my goop. I point outside. "Mmmm-mmmm-mmmm exchuzzzed sssss Niles?" I ask with a full mouth.

Mom shakes her head in mom-disappointment. "Fine. Be back in an hour." She shoos me out, probably grateful she and Delia can watch *Game of Thrones* or *The Bachelor* or some other violent nudity show without having to pause it when I walk into the room.

I grab the latest *Amulet* graphic novel off our entry table— Pablo asked me to give it to Niles—and stuff it in my hoodie

72

pocket. I'm halfway to his house before I finish chewing. Anyone who sees me sprinting to his house will probably think it's from the torrential downpour, instead of the life-or-death matter it is.

I'm soaked and hunched over from a side-ache when Niles's mom answers the door.

"Lupe. Get in here before you catch a cold." Mrs. Foster grabs me and pulls me inside.

I decide not to tell her there are no viruses in rain. The air inside the house is stuffy and smells like a campfire from a smoldering log in the fireplace. "Would you like to have a seat?" She motions to an antique couch with lions carved into the feet. Mr. Foster is slouched in his recliner next to the couch reading his *Dark Tower* series. He's still wearing his gi, which means he and Niles have been to their martial arts class at the dojo. Mr. Foster's been taking Niles since Niles was a Little Dragon himself.

I'd give anything to have what Niles has, a dad who makes sure he has the help and tools he says he didn't have as a kid.

Mr. Foster lifts his hand in a small wave to me. "Yeah, Lupe. Have a seat." He holds up his book. "Any interest in hearing how the human race screws things up for us this time?"

"No thanks, I watch the news. Just here to see Niles," I answer.

Mrs. Foster's forehead crinkles. "Is something wrong?"

"Not really. We just have a challenging assignment in one of our classes."

She quickly ushers me into the dining room that used to have all her scrapbooking supplies, but now holds an arsenal of essential oils in glass vials in a china cabinet. There are clinks as she reaches up to grab a tiny glass medicine dropper. The two rows of vials on either side tumble down, dropping like dominoes.

"Ah, here!" she says, squinting at the bottle in her hand. "Hawaiian sandalwood, peppermint, patchouli, and vanilla. My own blend, which I call . . ." She speaks in almost a whisper. ". . . *Encouragement*."

Before I can object, she's placing a drop on each of my wrists. "This will help." Then she drops a glop right on top of my head. "Now you're a walking diffuser."

"Great." I catch a whiff of myself. "Thanks. Sort of like if a holiday cookie were made of firewood."

She squints one eye. "Let me just get Niles for you. Niles!" she calls out again.

I've never asked a boy for something like this. Niles is different, though. He's like my brother. Still, my hands are sweating.

Niles's head pokes out like a tortoise from his bedroom door. "Hi Lupe," his head says after a few seconds, his body still hidden behind his door.

He steps out into the hallway. He's wearing new mustard-yellow-and-black footie PJs that bag around his ankles.

"Hey Niles," I say.

He smiles and walks into the dining room with us. He leans forward and sniffs. "Oh no, *Encouragement*," he whispers. "What's wrong?"

Mrs. Foster hasn't left yet. She's really nice but definitely one of those parents who's not afraid of listening in. "Can I get you two a snack?"

Mom's mystery pea goop is now roiling in my stomach, making awkward gurgles. "No thanks." Mrs. Foster glances toward a different shelf and I wonder if she has an oil called *Digestion*.

Thankfully, Niles chimes in too. "We're good, Mom."

"Well, then. I guess I'll let you two visit," she finally says and retreats into the kitchen.

Niles and I walk down the hallway to his room.

Niles points to the pocket of my hoodie. "What's that?" he asks, smiling.

I roll my eyes. "You know exactly what it is." I take the graphic novel out and hand it to him.

"Yes!" His eyes light up as he stares at the cover. "I've been waiting forever. Will you tell Paolo thanks for me?"

"Yeah, yeah." I glance over at Niles's graphic novels. He has them stacked by binding color so the towers of blue, red, yellow, and green look like mini skyscrapers. Boys like Paolo and Niles probably see those graphic novel piles as millions of worlds they can escape into. I sigh, staring at the brightly colored book buildings. "They don't even look like real books."

He gives me the faintest hint of a stink-eye. "Oh, these are real books, Lupe." He holds the book like a holy relic and sets it on his nightstand.

His martial arts supplies are in their usual spot on a chair on one side of his bed, his new brown belt and foam nunchakus draped over his white gi. Niles might seem pretty zen most of

75

the time, but I've been to a few of his belt tests, and let's just say I'm glad he's on my side.

Just to the left of his Bruce Lee *Enter the Dragon* poster is a framed copy of Niles's dojo's "Home Rules." Listed are rules like: "Always be truthful." "I will always be kind to all living things." "I will always finish what I've started." "I will always respect my parents, teachers, and elders." Niles likes these rules, and I get it. He actually goes out and lives them too.

But unlike Niles, I find some of the rules questionable. Like: "I will always tell my family good morning and good night." "I will always keep my room clean." "I will always help with household chores." "I will keep my hair, teeth, and body clean."

My mom asked Niles's mom for a copy of the rules for my room. I might've "lost" them.

A picture of Niles with the three-to-five-year-old Little Dragons also sits on his nightstand. Next to it, I see a neon-pink pad of Post-it notes that read "Great Work!", "Superstar!", and "Way To Go!", which Niles makes to put on the kids' foreheads after class. He sort of invented the notes, and apparently it stuck. Literally. Now the other instructors put the encouraging notes on kids' hands and foreheads too.

"Can I write one?" I ask.

He shrugs. "Sure."

I take the pen and write "There's no whining in karate!" on a Post-it.

Niles grimaces and pulls my attempt off the pad. He gently places it in the trash. "Maybe leave the inspirational notes to me."

I point to the *Star Trek* logo on his new pajamas. I wouldn't have noticed except that for the past six months, Niles has rotated between the *Doctor Who* Dalek and Hubble telescope jammies I gave him for his last two birthdays. "What's up with the new PJs?" I ask.

Niles glances toward his drawer. "Just something new."

I can't put my finger on why, but I feel a ping of nervousness. I hope this new interest is just temporary.

"I wanted to ask you something." I take a deep breath.

"What's up?"

"It's about the boy-ask-girl thing in P.E." Now on top of my palms sweating, my feet are getting hot. "I think I know of a way we can still help each other."

Mrs. Foster walks by the door and her footsteps stop. I know she's listening around the corner.

"Most of us don't really want to dance. So, if the boys have to ask the girls, wouldn't we all rather dance with a frieeeend?" I motion to myself.

"Does she smell?" he asks.

I lean toward my armpit and sniff. "Not important. Listen, I've thought about this." I lean in. "I mean me. You should just ask me."

He's closing one eye and his lips are pursed together. I haven't seen this expression before, so I'm not sure if it means he's got to go to the bathroom, or he's in deep thought.

I pat his shoulder like I've done for years. "Number one—if we have to dance, we should dance with someone we don't mind dancing with."

Niles rubs his chin. "That makes sense," he says.

I let out a deep breath, smiling. "Yes. And number two—you are the most agile person on two legs that I know."

He finally smiles back. "Okay then," he says. "I wasn't sure who I was gonna ask, but I guess it'd be fun to dance with you."

"So, it's a deal?"

He holds out his hand and we shake on it. "Deal."

"Is it cool?" I ask, which is our signal to see if I can give him a hug. He's explained that hugging feels different for him than something like a pat, or a high five, even if it's from a friend. It can be overwhelming, so he likes to be asked first.

He nods, and we give each other a quick hug.

I guess I never really thought about Niles asking another girl. There's definitely no other boy I'd want to dance with. But we'll be good together and (I tell myself) it will help both of us. I can meet Fu Li after all. Win, win.

I stand to leave and Niles walks into his bathroom. Within a few seconds I hear him brushing his teeth. He pokes his head out. "Night, Lupe," he mumbles with a mouthful of toothpaste. He closes the door again.

I grin as I pass his "Home Rules" chart: "I will always tell my family good morning and good night."

I walk out and nearly run into Mrs. Foster, who's pretending like she was strolling down the hall and hadn't been standing there for minutes. She smiles and gives me a squeeze before telling me to say hello to my mom.

I pass Niles's dad on the way out. Mr. Foster sighs and closes his book. "Clever man, King," he says, raising the book up to show me the cover.

I raise my eyebrows at the illustration of a dark figure with glowing eyes. "Not sure I could sleep after reading that," I say.

He smiles. "Same. I'll need to reset my mind a little. That's what this is for." He reaches down and pulls a different book from the side of his recliner. Its cover has setting suns behind a city twice the size of downtown L.A. "It's only a little less horrifying."

I laugh.

He smiles back. "Niles and I will read a bit from this before bed. Would you like to hang out and read with us?"

I want to answer yes but I'm already pushing my luck with Mom. "Wish I could, Mr. Foster. Mom said I have to get right back home."

"Well it's a standing invitation, Lupe. You're welcome to our family book club any time."

I feel a tightening in my chest. I mean, I wish I had my own dad back, but I'd take a dad like Niles's too.

He sets his book down and looks up. "Well then, night Lupe," he says, sounding so much like Niles.

I hope Niles is just like his dad when he grows up, so I have someone interesting to hang out with when we're super old like Mr. Foster and my mom.

I wave and shuffle out the door.

The rain has stopped. I take a deep breath. Success. My

mission to find a dance partner is complete. I run the whole way back, leaving a trail of vanilla-campfire-cookie scent in my wake and with a grin on my face.

It's not the perfect solution. We still have to dance, but Niles and I are doing it on our own terms.

CHAPTER 8

Must be a full moon or something. The halls are exceptionally dangerous for a Thursday. And on top of the paths being wet from a thunderstorm, someone has launched a beach ball. Now everyone is paying more attention to hitting the ball around than to where they're walking. Andy, Niles, and I walk out of the cafeteria. Andy stops to sort her trash into the recycling and compost bins, and Niles snags my arm before a kid barreling down the hallway launches me from the cement path into the surrounding mud.

Niles quickly lets go to adjust something on his endangered-Tenino-pocket-gopher T-shirt. Just above the buck-toothed rodent sits a pin in the shape of a slanted, filled-in gold letter *A*. I'm pretty sure it's another *Star Trek* thing.

Andy's sorting routine will take her just long enough for me to double confirm we're on the same page.

"Niles, just making sure, are we a go?" We have less than two minutes before we need to be in the locker room. After that, it will be radio silence until the boys have to ask the girls. That, and Andy's almost done sorting.

"Hey guys." Gordon is walking toward us and waving his hand like he's fanning a fire.

Perfect. Now I have to worry about square dancing enthusiast Gordon finding out about our pre-arranged partnership and telling Coach Solden. I continue, "You haven't forgotten—"

"Of course not," Niles says.

We're interrupted by Gordon lifting up his T-shirt and pulling it over his head. Darth Vader's face covers his own. I'm debating how I should react when he starts singing a muffled, "Dun, dun, dun. Dun de dun, dun de dun." He pulls the shirt back down.

Niles raises his eyebrows at Gordon and pushes the pin on his chest. It makes a little chirping noise.

Gordon laughs. "Touché, Crewman Niles."

The familiar ping in my stomach has returned. I tap Niles's arm. "Niles, do you think—"

But now, Niles is distracted. Gordon is brandishing something wrapped in foil in front of him. He holds it in front of his body making a *thv-thv-thv* noise. No one else could make that perfect whirring sound like Gordon with his missing front teeth. He unwraps the foil from what I now realize was an imaginary lightsaber and takes a bite just as Andy returns.

"What are you eating?" Niles asks Gordon.

"Just a little snack. Breakfast burrito," he says, taking a bite.

I decide not to mention that we literally just ate lunch. A piece of egg plops onto the ground.

"Gordon. It's 1:15," I say. "How long has that been in your backpack?"

"It's okay. Gram says I have an iron stomach." He pats his belly and then wipes a strand of cheese off his chin.

"Are old eggs and cheese a good idea right before P.E.?" Andy points out, nodding to the mangled glob in Gordon's hand.

"It's only a problem if I jump around. Besides, I know exactly which lucky lady I'm going to ask. We will be smoooooth on the floor." He circles his non-burrito arm in front of him and ends his move with a finger pointed right at me. A piece of egg fills in the gap of his missing front tooth.

Andy snickers and turns away.

Gordon's about to ruin everything. If he asks me first, I'll *have* to say yes.

"Listen Gordon, no offense . . ." I start.

Mom says when someone says "no offense," there's a pretty good chance they're about to offend you.

". . . but I'd rather you didn't ask me."

"But, but . . . you said you wanted an A. Gram and I have been practicing. I thought you and I'd make a good team." Gordon's hands are palms-up in front of him pleading with me.

I glance at Niles, but he clears his throat and turns away. And Andy is purposely avoiding eye contact with us too.

83

The warning bell rings and I have no more time to sort this out. I stop and block Niles and Andy's view. "Gordon. Do. Not. Ask. Me." I lean in and look him directly in the eye. "Got it?"

He closes his burrito wrapper and sets it in his backpack, looking down to avoid my eyes. His cheeks are suddenly splotchy. "Sure, Lupe. Sorry if I bothered you." He walks quickly away into the boys' locker room, his shoulders hunched forward.

***

Just like Gordon did, Samantha pulls the bottom of her gym shirt up as we get ready, but instead of pulling it over her head, she tucks it through the neck hole like a makeshift bikini. With most of Sammy Sockeye's body inside her shirt, all that's left is our mascot's smiling head and cartoony thumbs-up over her right boob. Claire and another one of Samantha's followers scramble to tuck their shirts through their neck holes too.

"Hey Guadaloopy. Anda-loser," Samantha says.

Andy tries to stand in between me and Samantha. "Don't," she pleads with me, but it's too late. My crappy comeback chip is already activated, and I'm on my tiptoes looking over Andy's shoulder.

"Hey yourself, Sam-o-nella." My attempt to emphasize the word just comes out more like a bad stutter-pun.

Samantha and her minions laugh. "Oh, good one."

Andy and I retreat in defeat to the gym. "Why do you do that?" Andy is half-laughing. "Seriously? Samonella?"

84

Coach blows her whistle three short times. Kids pile out of the locker room into the gym. Thirty seconds later she blows it two short times. It's like the middle-school version of a time-out countdown, but if she gets to one whistle and you're not out, you can get marked down. Samantha and the other bunheads saunter out.

Jordyn and a few club soccer girls come out together and walk by us.

"Hey Andy," Jordyn says, completely ignoring me.

"Hey Jordyn," Andy says back, waving awkwardly to them. I know she went to her first practice, but this is happening too quickly. My stomach swirls.

Coach sounds the final whistle and everyone's out . . . except Gordon. He finally skulks through the doors like a constipated camel.

"Hustle, Schnelly!" Coach yells.

He shuffles his feet a little, but he's not moving any faster. I hope what I said isn't getting to him.

"Samantha, Claire, Megan! Fix your shirts. We aren't going to a spring-break beach party."

I've never seen three people roll their eyes at exactly the same time. They pull their shirts down over their stomachs.

"Gentlemen. Over here." Coach points to the free-throw line.

"Ladies." She points to the out-of-bounds line. "Everyone, space yourselves out evenly facing someone on the other side." She claps her hands together over and over like a ticking clock. I stand between Zola Fimple and Andy.

If we were finalists in a beauty pageant, we might hold hands in solidarity. But the last thing I'd want to do is hold hands with Zola. Zola, a.k.a. the Green Goblin, is a serial nose-picker. Well, at least she was in the second grade, and old habits die hard. Even worse, she eventually found out I was the one who started the Green Goblin nickname and hasn't spoken a word to me since.

When everyone is in place, Coach rubs her hands together like she's hatched a plot to get every kid in America to love sit-ups and burpees. "So. The moment we've all been waiting for. Today we pair off with our dance partners."

Someone makes a gagging noise and the kinds of words you hear on the bus echo through the gym.

"That's enough." She faces the free-throw line. "Some of you might have heard the good news. The four best teams from each P.E. section get a coveted spot on the school stage during Issaquah Salmon Days and an automatic A in the class."

Maybe five people mumble excitedly, but most of us are staring at the opposite side of the room, more concerned that we're about to hold hands with someone of the opposite sex who is not our brother or sister.

"So, men. I suggest you ask someone you think you can partner well with."

The boys are glancing down the row like they're inspecting eggs in a carton. Some of the boys lock eyes on someone immediately. Gordon's scanning back and forth; his snarled half tooth is biting over his lower lip. I try to make eye contact with Niles, but he and Carl Trondson are distracted and pointing at a volleyball lodged impossibly into a light fixture near the ceiling.

"As we've learned in class, gents will extend your hand and make a small bow." Coach puts her right foot and hand out. She dips her head.

A wave of groans bellows from the boys' side.

"Settle down." She blows her whistle and it gets quiet again. "Ladies. It takes a lot of guts to ask someone to dance. After the invitation, you will take your partner's hand and move to the center of the gym until everyone has a partner."

Carl breaks ranks and limp-runs toward Coach. He almost trips in his rush. He hands Coach a note.

Her brow is furrowed as she attaches the note onto her clipboard. "Fine, Trondson. You sit this one out." Coach stares at her notes and shakes her head.

Carl takes a seat on the lowest bleacher. He makes a fist pump toward the boys while Coach is focused on writing something down.

Niles and I got this. Even on the days I have baseball practice after school, I'll have an hour before dinner to go to Niles's house to practice. We can at least make the top twenty percent and guarantee my A.

Coach blows her whistle again. This time it's louder and longer. She does her signature shirt tuck, and hikes up her shorts. "Let's get this started," she screams out like the pro wrestling announcer on TV.

87

At least two boys wipe their hands off on their shorts. To make the entire thing more humiliating, Coach hits play on her stereo. The instrumental version of "Turkey in the Straw" with fiddles and banjos strums out. This entire thing feels very wrong. I can't be the only one who has ever felt this way.

Blake struts forward first. He's got on his swagger like when he's coming up to bat. He walks immediately toward Samantha. No surprise she's going to be the first one asked. Her arms are folded and she flutters her eyes pretending to be annoyed, but she's bouncing up and down on her toes. He bows and holds out one hand.

Samantha takes Blake's hand. The side of her mouth makes a little upturn.

Blake makes an exaggerated wink back at the boys.

Samantha crosses one foot over the other like she's waltzing onto the dance floor at a recital instead of the center of the gym. She narrows her eyes right at me as she saunters by. She thinks she's won. But I know something she doesn't. No one is *making* me say yes. I'm *choosing* to say yes to Niles, on my own terms.

Blake has broken the seal, so now other boys walk forward to ask the girls. Some of the kids bow and accept before they're even within ten feet of each other. It's obvious a lot of kids have the same pre-arranged agreement Niles and I have.

There are enough gaps in the line now that Zola, Andy, and me are completely off on our own.

Over at the boys' end, Gordon stares at the ground and walks toward me, his chipped tooth shining under the gym lights. I thought I was clear. I can't believe he's doing this.

When Gordon's within a few feet, he holds his hand out to Zola. I loosen my clenched fist. Zola bows back and her braid almost touches the ground. She takes his hand.

Carl yells out from the sideline. "Hey look! It's Gordon-Zola! Get it? Like the cheese!"

The entire gym erupts in laughter. Even Coach smiles before she blows her whistle.

Gordon laughs too. Then, his face goes completely blank. He turns two shades paler than usual. His lips are purple and sweat beads up on his upper lip.

"What's wrong, Gordon?" Zola drops his hand.

Gordon clasps both hands over his mouth. His cheeks puff out like a chipmunk's. The entire class recoils in epic horror as a yellow sludge of emulsified egg and sausage spews through his fingers and onto the floor. Andy, Zola, and I all jump back but it's not fast enough to avoid some spray hitting our shoes. Sympathy gags spread around to other students. Even Andy is closing her eyes and taking deep breaths to avoid losing her own lunch, which is surprising for someone who specializes in owl puke.

Coach runs over and ushers Gordon away. She grabs the phone off the wall. "Wet mess in the gym! Code V!" Less than thirty seconds later, the janitor, Mr. Helms, runs in with a canister and starts dusting the yellow sludge with mystery powder.

"I'll be right back," Coach says. "You all stay put," she calls, leading Gordon out of the gym. It's silent for a few seconds while we all just stand around digesting what just happened.

"Krakatau!" Carl yells out and pretends to make a volcanic eruption explode from his mouth.

Nearly everyone laughs and starts chatting. Zola is staring down at a sausage chunk lodged in her shoe, muttering to herself, "Why is it always me?" Mr. Helms keeps sprinkling the granules but takes a second to point to his eyes then back at us in warning. Within a minute, he's sweeping up Gordon's breakfast.

Coach eventually comes back, wringing her hands together, and everyone quiets down. I catch a whiff of hand sanitizer as she passes me. She directs us to the opposite basketball key as Mr. Helms wheels in a metal bucket sloshing with pine-scented water.

Four of the five boys left use the chaos to walk over and ask their partners without an audience. Those couples jog quickly onto center court with everyone else.

Now that most of the class has been paired up, only a few of us are left. The earlier look on Coach's face now makes sense. Even before we're lined up, it's obvious we're one boy short.

Andy and I are the only girls left still walking toward the out-of-bounds line.

Standing on the free-throw line, alone, is Niles.

"Oh no," I whisper, but I know Andy hears me.

She hasn't been asked by association. Being my best friend has cost her again. Her chin is trembling, just like when she wet her pants.

90

"Andy . . ." I nudge her hand.

"It's okay. I don't care," she lies. Her head drops to her chest.

Niles is already walking toward me. This is my fault. Now there's no one to ask Andy to dance.

Niles marches forward. He stops right in front of us, and looks between our heads at the green foam wall-mats. Then, he's suddenly staring at Andy. I glance over too. Before she turns away, I catch a glimpse of a look on her face I've never seen before. As her chin trembles, she makes a hard wince like she's going to shut out the flood of embarrassment that's about to hit her.

This is awful, and I want it all to be over now. But Niles still isn't bowing.

Why's he hesitating? I reach out my hand, just a bit, to help move things along. When my hand is almost touching his, he notices, and looks at me. Then he takes a small step to the side and puts his arm out.

He bows . . . to Andy.

Andy and I turn our heads at the same time and stare at each other. I awkwardly tuck my hand behind my back. Samantha laughs so loudly everyone can hear her over the music.

Coach blows her whistle and quickly looks down at her clipboard. "Andy, you know the drill."

Andy glances at Coach . . . then me . . . then Niles. She bows back and takes his hand. Andy and Niles walk to the center of the gym with the rest of the class. My face gets hot.

As Coach changes the music, everyone is staring at me like I'm a blob-fish. Samantha cups her hand to the side of her mouth and says something. Her bunhead groupies and even Blake giggle. The singing version of "Turkey in the Straw" blares out in the background. The caller yells out, "Grab your partners!"

Well, I got what I wanted from the start. I'm not dancing. I try to breathe and it feels like my rosin bag is lodged in my throat. Isn't this what I was looking for? I tuck my hands in my pockets and step backward. I wish I could dissolve into the wall. Instead, I stand by myself against the green padding. I hope everyone is far enough away they can't see. A tear sneaks over my lower lid and down my cheek.

CHAPTER 9

Zola returns from the locker room smelling like hand sanitizer.

"Without Gordon, looks like the two of you get to dance together today," Coach says.

I open my mouth. Why now? Why couldn't Andy and I just dance together in the first place? Instinctively, I stare down at Zola's hands.

Zola must have seen my not-so-stealth inspection, because she glares at me and grunts like she's got a fur ball. I know it's a little hypocritical after I just rubbed the snot running down my nose. And how much damage could she have done between the Purell dispenser and here? The caller yells out for a promenade, and when Zola snatches my hand like an annoyed mother does with her toddler at a store, I trail along.

A few days ago, all I wanted was for square dancing to go

away. Now, I'd give anything to have Gordon Schnelly as my partner. He won't even be in science so I can apologize for how I spoke to him. Right about now he's probably in the nurse's office getting too-tight loaner sweats, waiting for his parents to pick him up.

Why the heck did Niles stray from our plan?

Zola squeezes my hand like I'm responsible for this whole square dancing fiasco. I spend the next twenty-five minutes on a sensory overload of hand cramps, body-odor winds, a kaleidoscope of twirling green-and-blue gym shirts, and some old guy screaming out instructions in a farm-ish accent.

***

Andy, Niles, and I walk in silence to our next class.

We come to our usual Andy drop-off spot. She stands in her doorway. "Sorry, Lupe."

I glance at Niles, but I don't think he heard.

Andy boops my nose and walks into social studies.

Niles and I lock elbows and we walk toward science class.

Mr. Lundgren has on a bright orange T-shirt with a smiling glass beaker. A dialogue bubble is coming from the beaker's mouth: "If you're not part of the solution, you're part of the precipitate."

Niles sets down his backpack and retrieves our lab materials before the bell has even rung. I sit with my elbows on the table, hands over my eyes.

The clinking of glass on glass mixes with students' voices. Niles mumbles, "Baking soda, calcium chloride, H2O, graduated cylinder . . ."

I peek out my fingers. Vials of solution are now lined up in a holder at our station, and Niles also arranged a pen and tape and a lab book in front of us.

Carl walks in and a few people clap. He sits at the station across from us.

I poke my head through the hole separating our stations. "How'd you get out of it? What did your note say?"

"Warts," he says, with a sneer on his face.

"What?" I ask.

"Plantar warts," he says. "I had two taken out of my heel."

I smack my forehead. "Why didn't I think of that?"

"It's not like I planned it," Carl's voice squeals. "It hurt."

"I call bull," I say.

He reaches in his backpack and pulls out a tiny sealed jar. Two grainy pebbles float around inside like decomposing cauliflower chunks.

"The doctor let me keep them."

Mr. Lundgren is peeking over Carl's shoulder. "Mmmmh. Formaldehyde." He says it like the jar is filled with a yummy treat.

"This is the worst day ever." I put my hands on my face trying to block out the world.

Niles sits down next to me. "Lupe, you're not upset I asked Andy to dance instead, are you?" he asks.

I peek between my fingers. Niles is swaying. Still, I can't answer or my voice might crack.

"I know we had a deal, and I know you need the A, but when I looked at Andy . . ."

I don't answer. I saw the same look on her face. I turn away just like she did so he can't see my eyes. He did the right thing, even if it kinda sucks for me now.

I guess the day could be worse—if I held it against Niles for just being a good person.

"Yeah, you did the right thing."

CHAPTER 10

At least baseball practice starts tomorrow, so I have something good to take my mind off what a disaster my life has become. After school, I'm in my backyard and have one bucket of balls left, which should be plenty to get to my eighty-one.

"Sixty-seven . . . Sixty-eight . . ."

I'm almost done. This is the point where my dad would've encouraged me through to the end. And these are the times I miss him most and imagine he's with me.

The pocket is blurry through my tears.

Focus. It's just you and me. Dad hits the center of his mitt with his other hand. *You got this, Lupe.*

I want him to really be here so I can run into his arms and tell him how bad my day was.

I hear someone walking down the alley. I hurry and blink away my tears.

Paolo walks up in his soccer uniform. For a second I wonder if he knows I'm upset.

"Sixty-nine," I say, keeping a straight face.

Paolo looks like he's going to pass by and leave me unscathed. Instead, he jukes and takes me out at the knees. The wind is knocked out of me a little. He hoists me back up by the waist of my jeans, giving me a wedgie. He strolls into the house like he didn't just lay me flat, and possibly hinder my ability to ever have children.

I shake my fist at him. "Someday, when you're old and in a wheelchair, I'm gonna push you down a hill, Paolo!"

"Good one!" he yells back. I've officially hit my second crappy comeback in a day.

I get set back up and readjust my jeans, throw the next pitch, and completely miss the strike zone. I throw my glove down and sit on the porch. This is happening because I'm letting square dancing beat me.

My dad stands. *You gonna let that one pitch defeat you, Lupe? Wongs don't give up that easy.*

How pathetic is it that I'm letting some old-fashioned dance mess with my game? I can't give up.

What did Delia say? Change.org seemed a bit extreme before, but desperate times . . .

I hear Paolo turn on the shower, meaning I have two or three minutes before he comes back out (smelling no better than

98

when he went in, I might add). So I have to get to the computer in the family room and type fast.

Attention, anyone with any humanity! The suffragette movement has come to Issaquah Middle School! Please help stop the barbaric practice of required square dancing in which girls have to say yes to male suitors! This is an antiquated custom and needs to end immediately. Like tomorrow before school starts! Please write in to Principal Singh (email copied below) to let her know how you feel.

Signed,
Anonymous Concerned Citizen

"Can't make it any worse," I mutter. I hit enter.

I spend the rest of the evening hiding in my room. I even do the "pretend to clean my room" trick. My mom won't want to thwart a miracle, so that will keep her from asking too many questions.

Finally, I crawl into bed, but my mind won't settle. I keep thinking of the Change.org campaign. I doubt myself and whether or not it was a good idea. I stare at the ceiling. Then I stare at my Fu Li card. That makes it worse. I imagine baby hedgehogs getting baths. Nothing helps. I take three deep breaths like Papa Wong tells me to do when I'm stressed. It sort of works. I close my eyes and feel myself drifting. It will be fine.

No one will even read it.

***

The next morning, I scarf down a stale concha and sit at the computer before school. I hit the envelope button for my email. Something's wrong. It normally loads in a few seconds and pops up showing a few overnight junk emails. This time it's at four hundred and twenty-three and not stopping. I think I've gone viral.

The subject line on the first email reads, "How cute! Go get 'em! You have my support!"

The second says, "Outrageous! Should we bring back petticoats and chastity belts?"

I'm not even sure what those things are.

Mom rounds the corner.

"Nothing!" I yell out and hit exit before she even asks what I'm doing.

"Okaaaay . . ." she says, shifting her eyes around in confusion. "You need to go. You're going to miss the bus."

My stomach swirls concha and milk, but not because I might miss the bus. I grab my backpack and run out, hoping my mom doesn't decide today's the day to start monitoring my email.

***

Principal Singh's voice crackles over the loud speaker during first period. "Ahem . . . I . . . uh . . . have received no fewer than two thousand emails regarding a certain school matter overnight."

I squint and cover my eyes. This is worse than I thought.

"It seems there is great concern over equal opportunity issues regarding square dancing," she says. "I agree. We need to change this."

I can't help the surprised little gulping noise I make, and the grin spreading over my face. I fold my hands in front of me on top of my desk. Mumbles go around the class. Two kids turn in their seats to look right at me, amazed looks on their faces. This is it! I'm about to become infamous.

"Therefore," she continues, "in addition to our already-established boy-ask-girl P.E. section, we will also have an entirely separate gender-neutral square dancing event."

My smile flattens. I tuck my hands under my legs. The astonished looks on the kids' faces shift to something more like a combination of a tetanus shot and hammer to the kneecap.

"This presents some scheduling issues. So this year, instead of the end-of-quarter Field Day, seventh graders will have a Sadie Hawkins, gender-neutral dancing day in the gym," she says excitedly. "Students will be able to ask whomever they choose!"

Someone pounds on a desk behind me. "Are you kidding me? Field Day is the funnest day of the year."

A pencil flies down the aisle and lands next to me.

"Now thanks to *someone*, we can't even have Field Day," Claire's voice chimes out. "I wonder who that could be?" I'm pretty sure the pencil flew out of her bun. I'm not even sure why Claire cares. Field Day is for sports. It's not like she can pirouette in between soccer and football players.

Principal Singh continues, "From this year onward too, square dancing in P.E. will be gender-neutral. There will be no more discussion on this matter." The intercom squeals then goes silent.

I'm staring straight ahead at the white board, but I can feel eyes all over me.

They all assume it was me. I mean, it was, but . . .

Ms. Craig pulls out her copy of *The Hunger Games*. "Turn in your books to page . . ."

I sit in class, pinpricks running over my face, waiting for the bell. I don't look up from my book and mostly forget to turn the page when Ms. Craig moves on. As Ms. Craig reads the book, there are gasps, oh-my-Gods, and cringes. But I can't even focus on any of what she's reading. The bell finally rings and I am up and out of my chair before everyone else.

I speed walk out, but Marcus runs out of the math class next door and blocks me in. "Nice work, Lupe."

I sort of expect this from Marcus. He's had it in for me since I beat him out for #1 in the rotation when we were nine. He wouldn't act like this in front of Blake or any of the others, though.

Now, the rest of my class is pouring out. And no one from the team is there to have my back.

"Thanks for ruining our lives!" Timmy Krueger bumps in to me.

His twin, Jimmy, stomps toward me and puts his face two inches from my cheek. "I heard she mixed Pop Rocks with Coke, so she has brain damage." His spit sprays into my ear.

"That's what happens when you go mixing things up," Timmy says.

I don't move, sort of hoping my instinct to play dead will make me less visible. My innards boil when I hear this kind of stuff, but my parents taught me to never react. I know better than to pick a fight with this kind of stupid.

"No, she's just naturally an idiot," Claire says, and they all laugh.

Niles exits LRC from across the hall. For just a moment I know they can't hurt me now. I loosen my grip on my backpack straps. I give Niles my most frantic "Help me" look and flick open my imaginary Sonic Screwdriver. He hurries over and takes my elbow, pulling me behind him. One leg forward, he bends his knees and projects his other hand pointed outward like a blade. He eases me away, like he's removing a carcass from a pack of stalking wolves.

Jimmy steps forward and tries to pull Niles away by his shoulder. Niles spins out of his grip and puts his fists up in a defensive position so fast everyone around us takes a step back. Jimmy's eyes go wide, almost like a cartoon character. He puts his hands up like he's warding off a werewolf. His voice cracks, "You better back off."

Niles steps back in front of me and reaches back, grasping my elbow again without taking his eyes off of them. Without a word, he leads me away.

Once we're a safe distance off, Niles lets go.

"Is it cool?" I ask, using our code phrase.

He nods. I put my arm around his shoulder and squeeze, then quickly let go before anyone sees.

Niles sighs. "Would you rather square dance with those people or eat ten banana slugs a day for the rest of your life?"

"Slugs," I say quietly.

CHAPTER 11

The twinges in my stomach must be like the itchy nose thing. Someone, somewhere, must be talking about me. But these pings are starting to feel like a bristle brush slamming against my insides. So *everyone* must be talking about me *everywhere*.

I haven't touched my sandwich once at lunch, and Niles is almost done organizing the raisins he's picked out of his ants-on-a-log by size. He licks the peanut butter off the largest raisin and pops it into his mouth.

I scan the cafeteria for Andy but can't find her.

Gordon sits next to us and opens his lunch bag. He dumps out all the contents and I can't help but notice there's an ice pack mixed in, to keep his food bacteria-free. He takes a swallow of an orange electrolyte drink, and his face twists up like someone's biting his big toe.

"Hey Gordon. How are you feeling?" I ask.

"Better, thanks." He puts an entire saltine cracker in his mouth. He chews for a solid thirty seconds, then dislodges a stuck cracker between his teeth.

"I'm sorry about how I acted yesterday," I blurt out. "I shouldn't have told you not to ask me." I glance at Niles pushing on a chip, flattening it. "It's just—I already had this plan . . ."

Gordon takes another drink of the orange stuff. He squints and shudders like it's vinegar. "It's okay, Lupe. You're good at stuff. I wanted a chance to prove to everyone I can be good at something too."

I push my chocolate milk toward him and take his electrolyte drink as a peace offering. "Well, you and Zola will have your chance today."

He looks up, his half tooth coated with orange cracker, and toasts me with the chocolate milk. "Thanks. I sure hope so."

***

Without a partner, I've prepared myself to clean bleachers with Carl or organize the ball closet in P.E., but Coach isn't there. Instead, an old man strolls out blowing a whistle, in a faded yellow tracksuit that looks like it hasn't seen the light of day in twenty years. A smile explodes across his face. His teeth are way too big to be his own.

"Attention, hooligans! *Miss* Solden isn't here today." His emphasis on *Miss* doesn't get by me. He lowers his voice . . . barely.

106

"I'm sure for some female reason." He clears his throat, and it sounds like he's gurgling mayo. "So, I'm your emergency sub today. I'm Coach Armstrong, and I ran the athletic program at North Seattle Middle School for forty years before I retired . . ." He chuckles a deep laugh. ". . . just a few days back." No one laughs with him.

All things considered, I'm pretty sure this guy hasn't seen an actual gym or student in fifty years.

"Today we'll be hanging up our hoop skirts and playing a man's game." He points to the whiteboard with "Capture the Flag" written on it. "Today, we go to war!"

There are whoops and fist pumps, but Gordon's entire body slumps into a C shape, like his spinal cord has turned to rubber. Even if I just caught a major break, I can't help but feel for him a little.

I try to make eye contact with Niles, but he's paying attention to the sub. He had to know about this change in our lesson plan. This isn't something Mr. Lambert wouldn't have cleared with him beforehand.

"To the team who wins, I'll make sure you get extra-credit points," Coach Armstrong says.

I'm not even sure if he's supposed to do that. But now, I'm going to need any extra points I can get. It might even push me into getting an A without needing to be a square dancing finalist. Fu Li, here I come! Even if this sub is a nimrod, Coach Solden won't go back on what he promised us. I have to win this game.

If I can get Blake and Niles on my team, it's a lock. I jump up to see over the crowd of kids to find Blake. I catch him glancing at me and he ducks down hiding. Marcus must have gotten to him. Even when we were little and it was our first year playing, Blake never shunned me. My dad said there was an unspoken rule on how a catcher always had their pitcher's back.

I yell-whisper with the stealth of a rhinoceros around the crowd, "Hey Blake!" I know he hears me, but he turns the other way. If Blake is ignoring me, the rest of the team is too. I'm on my own.

Coach Armstrong marches ahead and pumps an arm over his head. He shouts, "Hut, hut, hut . . ." Which I'm pretty sure is his confused version of a football call and marching orders.

I catch up to Niles. "Did you know about this?" I ask.

"Mr. Lambert asked me this morning if I was okay with Capture the Flag."

I make an annoyed grunt. "Could you warn *me* next time?"

"I thought you'd be happy," he says.

He's right. I've never asked Niles to tell me when he gets advance notice of a unit from Mr. Lambert. "I guess I should be happy. We just need to win."

We hike behind the track and up the trail to what used to be an archery field before someone accidentally shot an endangered prairie chicken. Now, the area is used for Scout campouts and Capture the Flag. It has a smaller, open central clearing but is surrounded by boulders and evergreens, making it the perfect battlefield.

Coach Armstrong counts us off by saying, "Hut, hike, hut, hike, hut, hike."

Not only is my plan to be on Blake's team ruined, but now I can't control who's on my team at all. I'm a hut. Andy's a hike, with Blake, Samantha, and Jordyn. But at least I have Niles.

"I've mixed things up a bit." Coach Armstrong holds up one red flag and one blue flag. Each has a round lump on the end. "I've wrapped a tennis ball in each of these. This, youngsters, will be a passing game." He mimics a long pass. "New rule! If you capture your opponent's flag, you can pass to a teammate. This will be a test of teamwork. If you get tagged, you're out. First person back to their own territory with the opponent's flag wins. Three minutes to hide your flag, starting . . . now!" He blows his whistle and tosses the flags, one to each side.

Andy waves back to me as she runs off with Jordyn. Niles, Gordon, and I run for our area and start searching for a good hiding spot. Zola insists it should be placed in a crevice making it more difficult to dig out. One kid uses up twenty precious seconds with a plan to keep it down his gym shorts and then toss it out when no one is watching. Niles raises his hand.

"Niles," I say, pointing to him.

Everyone leans in.

"They are going to come in there," he points to the center. "There," to another opening. "Or there." He points to a narrow passage I didn't even notice. "So we can't hide it anywhere along those lines."

It goes very quiet for a moment.

"So we should hide the flag where it's out of their line of sight on all three entryways," he adds. There are comprehending "aaahs" and "ooohs" from a few of us.

"And where would that be?" Zola juts her bony hip out so fast it looks dislocated.

Niles points to an outcropping of small rocks behind us. The one-minute warning whistle sounds.

I grab our blue flag and run it to Niles's spot. About half the kids don't even care about the game and run into the forest behind us. The only consolation is I know the same desertion is happening behind enemy lines on the other side of the field.

If we're going to win, I need a strategy. Send the fastest kids in. Keep the slowest on our front line to defend our area. Use the rest as decoys scattered in our territory.

Niles is faster than me, but in a game like this where people will be running and yelling, it might be stressful for him to run into the thick of it all. I run over to where he's standing, away from the others.

"What are you thinking, go after the flag or hang back here?"

He nods. "I was thinking backfield. It'll be quieter."

"You okay with tagging people? No worries if not."

"Better than being tagged," he smiles. "Let's do it."

"Awesome, we could use your speed!" No one is going to get past him with his jets.

We huddle up with the rest. "Zola, Niles. You two guard the outer fortress. Gordon, you stay on our side to guard our flag."

110

Gordon puts his palms up in front of him. "I can do this, Lupe. Just give me a chance."

I feel for him, and I just got done apologizing for being rude to him . . . but this isn't the time for Gordon to prove himself by being on offense. I need these extra points, and I'm not sure if I can trust him to run across into enemy territory.

"We need you to defend the Forest of Endor." I motion at the surrounding trees. "You are the perfect person to guard the magical hoard from the evil Orcs."

He tilts his head in confusion, then throws up his hands. "If that's what you think is best," Gordon says, moping back to the flag.

Niles is on the front line; legs squatted like a sumo wrestler, hands on his waist. He closes his eyes and is whispering to himself. I recognize it instantly as the meditation technique Niles uses to "get in the zone" before sparring. Zola glances over at him, then takes a deep breath and closes her eyes, doing the same.

A girl named Becca who runs track and two other boys are just standing around because they have no other choice. Even though none of them would act like they even know me out in the school halls, we all know what we have to do.

"What do you guys say, the four of us go in for the kill?" I ask.

"Whatever," Becca shrugs.

"We have to be fast," I continue. "They're probably going to send Blake in for our flag. I say we split up. If enough of us make it inside their camp, only one of us has to grab it. We can hot-potato the flag out of there with the new rule."

The two boys nod.

Becca yells to a few kids who are standing around in our territory without a job. "Use the boulders for cover! Tag enemy intruders!"

The whistle goes off. The four of us sprint out, scattering in different directions. The other team has just as many kids sprinting toward our side.

I'm the first to make it past their front line. Now I just have to avoid getting tagged so I don't go to jail.

Andy and Jordyn swipe at Becca and me as we run in. We weasel right by them. I look back to see they've tagged our two boys and are already leading them to their jail.

Up ahead, Blake is peering out from behind a tree. He sees me. He's not their runner, so this can only mean one thing. Blake's guarding their flag. He narrows his eyes at me like a puma. I know the look. He uses this glare on hitters when the count is 0-2, thinking he's intimidating them. He's letting his emotions get the best of him. I've just won.

I veer off to one side away from him, but I point toward where Blake is standing and yell to Becca, knowing their flag must be close to him. Instead of guarding the flag, Blake takes off after me. *Just* like I knew he would.

I let him gain on me then leap onto a boulder, scrambling over the top. I double back toward their flag. Becca's been tagged and is being led to jail. I have no backup so I'm on my own. But now, no one is guarding their flag.

A tiny piece of the red flag is sticking out of the dirt where

112

Blake had been standing. They've buried it (against the rules). But none of that will matter in ten seconds. Blake's breathing and footsteps are only a few feet behind me. I run by the flag and snag it between my fingers.

I'm looking for any other teammate for help, but all three of our fastest kids have been tossed in the pokey, along with almost everyone else.

I look to my opposite side and see Gordon. He's sprinting as fast as he can to catch up to me, but still falling behind. His eyes are wide and he's holding out wiggling fingers, "Here, Lupe!"

He's completely abandoned our flag, leaving Niles and Zola alone to guard our territory and the flag he's left unattended. He has the same desperate look in his eyes he had earlier, telling me how he just wanted a chance.

If this is what he needs to prove himself . . .

He's all I have, and Blake is right behind me.

If Blake tags me, it's all over.

"Gotcha!" Blake yells. But it's too late. The flag is out of my hands and flying toward Gordon.

Blake tackles me (also, against the rules). I fall hard but the ground is mushy with moss. I push myself up so I can see the show.

Gordon is pumping his arms so high he looks like he's leading a band. Except his legs move in tiny steps like they're tied together. It's not pretty, but he's got no opposition. He can make it. He glances over his shoulder, mouth so wide he has three chins and one of them is touching his chest. Then . . . with no

113

one even remotely within twenty feet of him, Gordon's arms start to windmill, his body lurches forward, and his feet tumble across each other like a hand mixer. He face-plants in a marathon skid, but he's still got the flag.

Samantha jogs over and "accidentally" pins Gordon's arm down with her sparkly sneaker. She stares at him like she's just stepped barefoot on a cockroach and snatches the flag from his hand. "I got it!" Just as she says it, a shout echoes from behind a tree in our territory.

Jordyn appears from behind the tree, a blue flag gripped in her fist. Without Gordon guarding it, she's found a way to sneak in.

Jordyn sprints like a gazelle toward Niles, who rises slowly from his squatted pose like Godzilla out of the ocean. At the exact moment she passes him, Niles jumps out, making an impossible launch through the air. Like something out of a movie, his hand arrowheads out to tag her, his body perpendicular to the ground. There are roars of triumph from our side.

But Jordyn has simultaneously thrown our flag toward her territory. Coach Armstrong doesn't blow the whistle, which means the game is still on. The sub smiles like a smug banana in his yellow tracksuit. Niles is already back on his feet.

I follow the blue flag as it soars high in the air, and right into Andy's hands.

It's too late. Niles is too far to catch her.

Andy's waving our blue flag as she runs. She's halfway to their boundary line in the same amount of time it took Gordon to fall. Andy spikes the flag inside their territory at their base. Samantha and Jordyn high-five her. Yells echo through the field and trees.

Andy runs over to me with a huge smile, sweat dripping down her face, and boops me on the nose.

CHAPTER 12

"Sorry, Lupe. I didn't even think about it," Andy says.

"Obviously." I don't even slow down, heading straight from the Capture the Flag catastrophe into the danger of a busy hallway day. "It's almost like you *want* to humiliate me on top of everything else I've been through."

"Are you being for real right now?" she says, stopping at her classroom door.

I poke myself. "I sure feel real. But you . . ." My mind flashes back to her high-fiving Samantha and Jordyn. I reach out and boop her a little too hard on her nose. ". . . feel like a joiner."

Andy puts her hands on her hips. Her nostrils flare. I've never seen her this mad.

Maybe if I'd been more open with her about how much I miss Dad, and why meeting Fu Li is so important, she would have remembered to let me win for the points. My heart is speeding up, but I narrow my eyes and lift my chin. She's the one who's suddenly trying to impress Jordyn and Samantha.

"You know what?" Andy says. "You're a whiner and you're selfish, Lupe."

"I'm selfish? You're the one who just *had* to show off with your new friends and win the stupid game."

Her head is either steaming from all that running on a cold day or actual steam is really coming out of her ears.

"Lately, all you care about are your own ridiculous causes," she says. "I'm starting to wonder if you just use everyone around you to get what you want." Andy's cheeks are suddenly darker. "Have you ever thought that other people might have issues and need good grades too?"

I think she's talking about stuff with her mom. But, her *issues* with her mom are not going to change anytime soon, and my getting to meet Fu Li is a little more pressing at the moment.

"I thought you wanted to help me get an A," I say.

Her hands are on her hips and she juts her chest out. "Well, your mom is a teacher. She can pull strings to get you help, unlike the rest of us."

I squint and lean in. "How soon you forget who covered for you when you peed your pants." I don't mean to say it as loud as it comes out. But it's too late, and a few kids turn and laugh.

Andy takes the tiniest step toward me. "At least I don't smell like dugout and jockstrap."

Now *my* nostrils flare. I know I should stop, but . . . "My mom

117

might talk to other teachers, but you can't even stand up to yours. I'll be halfway to the majors and you'll still be kicking soccer balls and writing computer code just to make her happy."

Andy's hands drop to her sides and she stares at the ground. She won't even look at me.

There's only one tiny snicker from one of the bunheads; then everything suddenly goes way too quiet.

When Andy looks up, her face looks like an abandoned dog's.

The kids are still watching. Why am I not taking it back? She's picking at her nail.

I'm waiting too long.

"You know what, Lupe? Go find a new best friend." She throws the owl sweatshirt I gave her for her birthday on the ground.

Niles backs away, swaying. He's shifting from one foot to the other, and now I feel even worse.

Andy stomps into her classroom, leaving me and him in an awkward silence.

What did I just do?

The back of my neck is suddenly flaming hot, and my chin starts to tremble. I try to make it stop by biting the inside of my cheeks. Niles and I stand off to the side in the hall until he's no longer swaying and I stop shaking. While the wait helps Niles, it just gives me more time to feel horrible about what I've done.

The warning bell rings and Niles nudges me. "Lupe?"

I don't look at him, afraid I'll break down in front of him. He digs into his backpack. He's quickly pulling something out and

118

unwrapping it. He lifts it up to my mouth, and I smell something amazing.

"What is this?" I barely get out before I take a bite and instantly taste something sweet.

"Dark chocolate. It really helps." Niles gently pulls at my elbow, and we walk in silence to science class.

The classroom is dim, and it takes a second for my eyes to adapt. But I'm thankful for the darkness so no one can see my face. And the chocolate really does help.

Mr. Lundgren is setting up a video of what has to be less boring than his lessons.

Gordon is standing at our station, hands cupped on his cheeks. "Sorry I blew the game for us," Gordon says. "They aren't broken in yet." Gordon motions to his brand-new sneakers.

I was so focused on the game, I hadn't even noticed his new neon-green tennis shoes. If my shoes had a little splatter after his breakfast-burrito explosion, his must've been soaked. He plops down in his chair, taking quick breaths.

I've never seen Gordon this upset. I knew he wanted to do good, but I didn't realize that Capture the Flag was so important to him. His goggles start to fog up. His face is normally kinda blotchy so I can't tell if he's hot and hyperventilating, or crying. This is all because of me. This day has gone from horrible to mass destruction. Gordon looks even worse than I feel right now after what happened with Andy.

I lean in to see if he's okay. "Next time we'll try to pass a little sooner." How is this happening again? I can't do anything right.

I pat him on the shoulder, even though we've never been close. "I know you wanted to win at something. You shouldn't be so upset though. It's just a game."

Gordon's brow scrunches over the top of his goggles. "Huh?"

"You're upset about Capture the Flag, right?" I ask.

He snorts. "Of course not. I'm used to losing at team sports."

"Oh . . ."

Gordon breathes in through his mouth. His lower lip makes that stuttery *f-f-f-f-f* noise. At this rate, he's not going to recuperate in time to be quiet during the video, the title of which is now projected on the screen: "I'm a Little Quarky—A Subatomic Particle's Confession."

"Umm, do you want to talk about it?" I say.

"It's my grandma . . ."

"Oh no. Something happened?"

"Yes," he wipes his nose with his sleeve. "The worst thing you could ever imagine."

And I thought what just happened with Andy was bad. Poor Gordon. "I'm so sorry. Why are you even here? You should be with your family."

He turns toward me. "Why would I need to do that?"

"Your grandma didn't . . . uh . . . die or something, did she?"

"No." He stands and takes a dramatic step back. "Worse. She got a boyfriend." He grabs his pencil by both ends and tries to snap it. When it doesn't break, he sighs and throws it on his composition book. "She took *him* to the senior center to dance last night instead of *me*. On top of that, Zola won't practice with me after school. She says she doesn't trust my gag reflex. It's the worst week ever."

"Sorry about your grandma falling in love," I say. "But maybe this can be okay." I don't know anyone more enthusiastic about dancing than Gordon. He might just be the perfect partner. And if Zola won't dance with him . . .

"How?"

"You were right. We would make good partners," I say. "What if I was your partner?"

"What about Zola?"

"I'll practice with you. She won't. We'll tell Coach that Zola isn't pulling her weight."

Gordon's head ambles back and forth like a turtle checking for traffic. "I don't know . . ."

I debate pulling the Zola/Green Goblin thing with Gordon, but he doesn't seem the type to care about boogers. What angle would work best with him? Maybe Andy was right about me using people to meet my goals. But what if I'm doing them a favor, too?

"Listen, you want to prove you're good at something. I need to find a partner who can get me onstage during the Salmon Days assembly," I say. "We can even practice this weekend."

His eyes light up.

"I have my first baseball practice today, but after dinner, you can come to my house," I say. "I'll even provide snacks."

He finally smiles and gives me a thumbs-up. "All right, but I need to recondition my stomach lining. Do you have anything rich in probiotics?"

It's been a pretty horrible day so far, but I have hope now that I'm dancing with Gordon.

CHAPTER 13

My first baseball practice sucks.

The red dirt is still damp from earlier rain, and the chalk lines are hard and grey. The cut grass is soggy enough to where I can't smell it.

Our new coach, Coach Frankie, starts with his bullet points of "disclaimers."

1. Miss more than three practices and lose your starting position for the season. We don't play that many games, so this is a big deal. You start, you get to play in the biggest games. (I can't think of anything worse than losing my #1 spot to Marcus and having to listen to him gloat. Even if I get Ebola, I'm not missing a single practice.)

2. No metal cleats.

3. Only approved batting helmets.
4. Mandatory athletic supporters for all players.

I raise my hand at the last one to tell the coach that the last time I checked, I wouldn't be needing one of those. No one laughs with me, and the coach just turns a shade pinker. I'm pretty sure this means Blake and Marcus have fully gotten to the rest of the team.

Coach Frankie decides we need to take our conditioning up a notch this season, so we have to run a mile before we even play. Normally Blake and I run together, leading the rest. But today, he purposely falls behind. No one else will even look me in the eye so I jog ahead alone.

Blake breaks the ice halfway through our second lap. "Thanks to *Lupe*..." He yells ahead. "... we don't even get to have Field Day."

"My mom keeps making me dance with her, and it's all *Lupe's* fault," Marcus says.

I turn and run backward. "How is that my fault? I didn't invent square dancing."

They push past me and keep running. Some things aren't worth arguing. I'm pretty sure if Blake or Marcus got lice from the batting helmets, it would somehow be my fault. I fall back, running behind them until we finish our laps and take the field.

No one covered the mound so there's a tiny puddle in front of the rubber. I kick water out with my foot and some seeps into my cleat. Just before I throw each warm-up pitch, Blake starts to shift his mitt off to one side. I still hit the zone each time.

Marcus saunters up to the box and hits the bottom of his cleat with the bat even though there's no caked mud yet to knock off. Blake pushes up his catcher's mask and whispers something to Marcus. They both laugh. He narrows his puma eyes at me.

I hear Dad's voice from behind me and the mound. *Don't let them rattle you.* I know he's not real, but still it calms me down.

Blake signals for a fastball.

I throw one down the middle and Marcus tips it off.

It's just you and the catcher, Dad says.

What my dad's voice in my head doesn't know is that the catcher right now is not on my side.

You don't have to be the fastest. Look at Moyer, he continues. I've heard this spiel before. Along with Fu Li, and Randy Johnson and a couple others, Jamie Moyer was one of the best pitchers the Mariners ever had. And he wasn't the fastest. He was pretty old even. But he was smart. He threw a killer changeup.

Blake throws the ball back to me, but high and to my left so I have to jump way off to one side, my glove barely catching it on the lip.

He has the nerve to signal for another fastball down the middle. I hope he's wearing his supporter today. I throw it inside and in the dirt. Marcus still swings and misses. Blake barely scoops it up and gives me a look.

I shrug. I know they're somehow setting me up, but I can't tell if Blake is on to me yet.

Normally, I'd just waste a fastball next outside one of the corners, to see if Marcus would chase it. But thanks to Blake, who's supposed to have my back, Marcus will be expecting it. I grip my fingers into a four-seamer.

Center your weight on the rubber, my dad says.

I step onto the mound, pushing my cleats down in front to balance on the balls of my feet.

Don't show 'em your cards.

I put my hand into my glove where they can't see I've slipped my grip back. I cup the ball to make a circle with my thumb and pointer finger, and put my middle finger down the center. Just like Moyer.

Blake shifts his glove to the outside corner of the box. Just like I knew he would, he signals for a fastball on the outside corner. Do they really think I don't notice Marcus moving toward the plate? I nod and keep a straight face.

I tune them out and listen only to my dad's voice. *It's 0-2. Think, Lupe. Command is as important as speed. Pick the right spot for this batter.*

Marcus is a decent hitter, but he only likes to pull. *Low and outside,* I answer my dad in my head. I take a small step back and center my weight.

Be deliberate in your windup, Dad says.

Yep, I answer. I lift my hands to my head, making sure to hide my grip on the ball. I bend back for balance.

Dad's voice is clear. *You got this.*

I let it go.

What they don't expect . . . my circle change is at least ten miles per hour slower than the previous pitch. Marcus swings.

A second later the pitch crosses the plate low and outside. Even Blake is caught off guard, has to do a double clutch to get his mitt on it, and drops the ball. He scrambles to pick it up.

"What was that!" Coach Frankie yells. "Blake, you need to be in tune with your pitcher."

They are too sheepish to even glare at me, but if they had, they would've seen my teeth gritting.

I'm still first in the rotation. I won't let them break me. This will only make me better.

***

I jump in the shower at home and barely have enough time to scrub off the muddy, red dirt rings around my ankles. I greet Gordon at the door. He makes a deep bow and when he straightens back up, his eyes are squinted shut from his chipmunk smile. Any other time I might think it's silly. But after what's going on with Andy . . . and my entire baseball team, I sorta want to give Gordon a hug.

I bow back. This will be worth it when Coach lets us be partners.

Of course, Gordon passes over the cacao-and-coconut probiotic bar I got for him. We finish our Cheetos and lemon-lime Otter Pops, and I try not to imagine the color of sludge that might come back up if Gordon jumps around too much. Then we get set up in the living room with "Turkey in the Straw" blaring out of the old computer speakers.

We face each other and hold hands. Gordon makes a formal bow that looks like we are about to waltz instead of square dance. I make a quick bow back. We begin with a swing, followed by the promenade. We each put out our heel, then toe, then promenade again. Gordon goes right and I go left. Everything is going well, then . . .

Gordon flings one arm straight out as he pops me under his arm.

"Gordon! That's not part of the routine."

He throws his leg and arm out even further, making a jazz hand. "It's called flourith."

"Flourish?"

"Yeah, flourith." He lifts his hands like pointed swan wings and looks toward the sky. "Grandma says great dancers aren't great because of their technique, they're great because of their passion."

"But there are rules." I say, hoping we won't get marked off for Gordon's ad libs.

"Well, the rules are debatable. And if I'm going to be your partner, Lupe, I suggest you keep up with the flourith," he says, dipping me.

My stomach dips with the rest of me. But I'm desperate. So if this is what I have to do to get my A, I will take some Pepto-Bismol and let Gordon flourish.

***

After a weekend of practicing with Gordon, I'm flourished out. But if the cost of having Gordon as my partner is a little motion sickness, it's worth it.

Monday morning, Coach Solden is drinking her morning coffee when I walk in. She sets down her Starbucks cup—it has "Bucky" written on it instead of "Becky"—and clears her throat. I can already imagine how they're going to butcher my name someday.

"Well, I'm starting to think you need your own desk in here. Can I offer you a cup of joe?" she asks.

This might go better than I'd thought. Grown-ups drink coffee with each other when they discuss stuff as equals. I look around for a mug. "Really?"

"Nah." She laughs like she's just made a hilarious joke. "But you can have some water out of the fountain." She points to the community spit-swapper.

"No thanks," I say.

Gordon still isn't here, even though we agreed on meeting at 7:54 sharp. It barely gives us six minutes to present our case. The clock clicks to 7:56.

"Can I assume this visit has something to do with the new gender-neutral policy from your Change.org campaign?" she asks. "I mean, it makes sense. If we'd had this when I was..." She glances off like she's seeing something I can't. She shakes her head like she's erasing an Etch A Sketch. "Let's just say I think you got this one right."

"That policy doesn't even start technically until next year," I say. "And how do you know it was me?"

Coach tilts her head to one side and smiles. She knows.

"But that's not why I'm here." I scan the field outside her window. Still no Gordon.

"Oh?" She sets her cup down. "I'm on pins and needles waiting to hear what you have up your sleeve now."

7:57. I can't wait for Gordon any longer. "So, let's say someone isn't happy with their choice in partners, and they want to switch."

"Nope," she says without hesitating.

"But Coach, what if the boy's other partner isn't enthusiastic about square dancing?"

She laughs. "Really? Says the girl who single-handedly got an eighty-year-old policy changed because she's so enthusiastic about it."

She's got a point. Partnerless again, I sag into the chair.

"Listen Lupe, life presents us with a few hurdles. But hurdles are there to make us jump higher." Coach is suddenly very focused picking something off the rim of her cup. "Even with something as fun as square dancing, there's always someone left out."

I squint at the spot on her mug where she's picking, but there's nothing there.

"I'm sorry about Carl," she says. "I didn't plan on that."

"Not sure anyone ever plans on warts, Coach. So, what now? I'll be running instead, right?" Getting an A and meeting Fu Li will be impossible even if I run all class. Fu Li was within my grasp, but now . . . "Is there anything I can do to get extra credit? Scrape gum off the bleachers? Scrub scuff marks off the floor?"

"What are you talking about? You're still going to be dancing. I only said there's always someone left out."

"You said to get an A—"

Coach interrupts. "Oh, you can still get an A. But you're not going to steal someone else's partner."

The sound of my name echoes like a tiny mouse screaming through a straw. "Lupe!"

I look in the direction of the scream. From across the track outside, Gordon is pumping his arms but running like his legs are superglued together again. He stops, pulls out his lunch sack to dump all the contents on the ground, and starts breathing in and out of the bag.

Coach stands and bows toward the wall. She starts prancing around like a magical unicorn at a Renaissance dance, pretending to hold someone's hand and twirling the imaginary person around.

Even though she's not my favorite person right now, it makes me sick to my stomach to watch her disgrace herself like this.

She finally stops mid-clomp and turns to me. "Ever heard of an invisible partner?"

I can't feel my toes.

I can just imagine the crap I'll get from everyone in P.E. for curtsying to the air. I jump up from my seat. "Please, Coach. I'll run all class long. Every day."

The bell rings and Coach walks toward the gym. "You're an

131

athlete. A strong will to learn is just as important as strong muscles, squirt."

She leaves me alone in her office. I'm no squirt. I reach over and grab Coach's cup.

I take a huge gulp . . . then promptly jump up and spit it into the garbage can. Maybe I'm not *that* grown up.

Why would an athlete need to have a strong will to learn square dancing when there are perfectly good sports to play? All I know is I'm still dancing alone.

CHAPTER 14

Gordon, Niles, and I settle in at our usual table in the cafeteria. Andy passes right by us without even a glance. She sits at the table with Jordyn and the soccer kids. She starts sharing her chips with Jordyn. It's the first time in four years Andy and I haven't shared our lunch.

In between bites, Gordon explains to Niles how he uses counting to help him keep his rhythm while learning a new dance.

"Could I count in Klingon?" Niles asks, putting his new *Amulet* graphic novel away in his backpack and giving Gordon his full attention.

"Whatever system works." Gordon counts in what I can only assume is Klingon. "Wa', cha', wej, loS." He smiles. "See. That's the beauty of music and dance. It works in any language."

They move on to discussing animals called tauntauns and

banthas, but I tune them out completely after the talk shifts to the banthas' herbivore diet.

My best friend won't even look at me. My other best friend appears to have a new friend. My teammates are annoyed with me. I have to air dance in front of everyone.

It can't get any worse.

I bet throughout history, everyone has wished for P.E. to disappear at least once. I never have. But today, I wish as hard as I ever have for an earthquake, zombie attack, or an overflowing toilet. Still, fifth period arrives.

Andy gets dressed in silence, her back to mine. Of course, I forgot my shorts again, and I can't ask Andy. I pull on the scratchy loaners. I'm not saying I wouldn't do almost anything for Andy's extra shorts, but I miss Andy way more than her shorts. This is what Papa calls a life lesson. Although suddenly losing your best friend on top of sandpaper wedgies is sort of a harsh way to learn you can't use people, or forget about their feelings too. I reach out to tap her on the shoulder, but she makes a quick eye roll at me before she slams her locker and runs ahead.

"Hey Jordyn," Andy calls out, disappearing into the gym, leaving me behind.

I look around the locker room, suddenly self-conscious without her. I fold my arms over my chest and walk out into the gym feeling very alone.

Coach pairs us off in five groups—four sets of partners in each section. Naturally, I end up with Samantha and Blake first. We all face each other. Me, the only partnerless person.

How hard can this be? I hold the records for pull-ups, shuttle run, and the peg wall. Those are all individual tests too.

Samantha's eyes shift to my shorts. "Let me guess. Goodwill?"

I really need to pull them down in the back, but this might not be the best time.

The music starts, drowning out her voice, but I clearly hear Samantha ask Claire if stupid is contagious.

"Grab your partners!" Farmer John hollers out just like he does every time the song starts blaring. The words echo loudly in the gym. I glance at Niles, who hurries to put in his earplugs. Blake and Samantha take each other's hands. My stomach churns and I'm happy my mom doesn't make breakfast burritos. I reach my hand out like everyone else, but mine is dangling midair. Do I wrap my fingers around an imaginary hand? I hold my fingers straight, then try curving them. Samantha and Claire see me and laugh, so I flex my fingers like they're sore and I was doing it on purpose.

We start with a promenade. I think about dancing with Gordon the night before and anticipate what's coming up. I'm going to have to twirl next, hand over my head. Not only will I look like one of those goofy plastic ballerinas in a jewelry box, my shorts will ride even higher.

If I don't have a partner, what will it matter to Coach if I lead? I quickly jump to the other side. We bow to our partners and line up across from one another. Banjos twang out, and one couple at a time we go to the center do-si-do. Without someone to lead, I guesstimate when to back up. I smash right into Claire.

"Watch it, klutz!" she says.

When I'm in the middle with my elbow out, spinning around an imaginary partner, everyone laughs. Blake actually winces. I know he's angry with me. But the look on his face right now is worse than if he were laughing at me. I think he might pity me.

The caller yells out, "Switch partners." For one twirl, I'm with Samantha. Now Blake has to pretend he has a partner. But it's not the same. He has someone to go back to in a few seconds, and no one's laughing at him.

Samantha and I are locked at our elbows, spinning in a circle. She glides around, her feet barely touching the floor. My feet hit the ground with thuds. It's not enough time for her to insult me, but she reaches up with her arm still connected to mine and pinches her nose.

Claire laughs, and when we switch again she does the same.

Now it's caught on, and every time I have a new bunhead as a partner, they pinch their noses too.

"Word is her parents found her at the dump," Samantha whispers in the loudest whisper ever. "That's why she smells like blowout diaper."

The caller yells out, "Ladies and gents. Weave the ring."

Now, I'm right next to Niles and Andy's group, so I know Andy can hear what's going on. Niles is counting in Klingon along with the music, so between Gordon's method and the earplugs he's too focused to notice Samantha's comments.

But Claire talks loud enough where everyone in our group

can overhear. "Science experiment gone wrong. Almost too short to be human."

I've learned to ignore comments and people like that. But when I see Carl scraping gum and dried loogies off the undersides of the bleachers . . .

I'd give anything to have his foot warts right now.

I don't even hear the caller anymore. I slam into someone behind me and stomp on their foot. Whoever it is screams. I turn around and Samantha is grabbing one foot and hopping around. She stares at the scattering of jewels on the floor.

"These are Pinnacle Stardusts!" Samantha jumps down and collects the pink jewels like they're diamonds.

"Get up, Pinkerton!" Coach yells. "And wear gym shoes from now on."

The song ends, and we move to another group of four couples. This time I'm with Gordon and Zola. I can breathe again. Even if I'm not Zola's favorite person, she doesn't want to kill me.

If only I could be dancing with a flourishing Gordon instead of holding an invisible hand and tripping over my own feet. We switch partners and I'm with Zola. It comes to the part where we're supposed to circle around one another. Mid-circle I accidentally pummel Gordon and he falls to the floor. I scramble to help him up. Coach sees me and jots something on her clipboard.

We switch for the final time and at last I'm with Andy and Niles. Niles counts, "Wa', cha', wej, loS," the entire time. It's addictive, and I catch myself saying the numbers in my head.

He's holding Andy's hand, which means he's comfortable with her.

When the caller yells out for us to switch, Andy puts out her hand, but she won't look at me. Her hand is limp in mine. I may as well be dancing with a wet mop.

Even when Niles dances with my pretend partner, he is in perfect time using Gordon's counting suggestion. But when they switch back, he accidentally steps on her foot.

"Ouch, Niles!" Andy yells like she's reprimanding her younger brother.

Niles flinches back.

I reach out to pat him. But before I can, Andy puts her hand on his shoulder and her voice turns notably softer. "Sorry. It's just, I have a hangnail."

By the end of class, the two of them are saying, "Wa', cha', wej, loS . . ." together and laughing. Something in my throat clamps tight.

We retreat to the locker room, and I'm so distracted I almost hand Andy the school's loaner shorts out of habit. She has her back turned to me, and I overhear Jordyn say something about getting açaí bowls after soccer practice. I can't take it! The Andy I know would never eat antioxidants for fun.

Andy slams her locker and walks out. I have to talk to her.

I'm running after her when Coach's voice echoes in the locker room. "Lupe, can I have a word?" She motions me into her office.

Andy walks ahead toward the main halls.

Did Coach figure out I drank out of her coffee mug? I fidget with my backpack.

"Don't worry about being late to your class. I'll give you a note," Coach sets her clipboard down and taps on it with her pen. "Not as bad as you thought it would be, was it?"

Does she even know how disastrous that was? "This is torture," I say under my breath.

"You're a strong kid," she says. "You and I both know you haven't had it easy."

I recognize the look on her face. It's the one people gave me after Dad died. So I'm pretty sure Coach is talking about that and not all the stuff with Samantha and Claire. I don't think she even sees most of the stuff they do in class.

She scribbles my tardy excuse on a note, rips it off the pad, and hands it to me. "Because I know how strong you are, I have faith you can do this."

CHAPTER 15

Our drizzly walk home is silent except for the *click . . . click . . . click* of Niles and me kicking our rock. I know Niles is a better listener than me, but I never realized how much more I must talk and how much more Niles must listen.

I'll try to be a better listener to my friends from now on. But today, all I can think of is Andy's silent treatment . . . and the things Samantha and Claire said . . . and how no one, including Andy, stuck up for me. The sadness makes me walk way slower than usual.

The one day I could use her, there's no sign of Delia in her yard.

We get to my gate and our rock ricochets into the gutter. I bend over to pick it up and see another rock caked in mud. It's the perfect size and shape for a mini landscape boulder in a mouse village. I polish it between my fingers and put it in my pocket for safekeeping.

The day's been pretty bad, so I hesitate before asking Niles, too afraid of the answer. "*Doctor Who* tonight?" I finally squeak out.

"So, I've been meaning to ask you, how about a marathon instead this weekend?" he replies. "We'll have a few episodes to catch up on." He hesitates for a moment. "And . . . I sort of made other plans again for tonight."

I know he has other friends at his dojo. But they don't live near us, and he's never let them come between us before. I bite the inside of my cheek to keep my chin steady. I know it's going to be sore, and it had just finished healing from when I bit it during my run-in with Andy.

"I'll even try to sneak us extra ice cream," he says.

I shrug. "Sure," I say, and walk up my driveway.

At the top of my drive, I watch him until I know he's almost to his house. Just before he reaches his door, he turns back and waves, and I wonder if we'll ever have our Monday nights back.

***

"How long will Grandma and Papa Wong be here?" Paolo asks. "I have this thing . . ."

Mom switches the music from Missy Elliot to classical as she rushes around the kitchen getting ready for our monthly dinner visit from my grandparents. "You don't see them as often as you should. Seeing you two makes them happy."

"Grandma's just going to yell at us for using too much soy sauce. 'Tchhhh,'" I say, mimicking her. "'Too much soy sauce!'" Paolo laughs.

"Be respectful." My mom's voice cracks. "You can't know how long you'll have someone." She makes the sign of the cross and sniffs.

Paolo and I finish setting the table without being asked, and no one brings up the soy sauce again.

Grandma and Papa Wong don't really cry or talk about Dad much, unlike Mom, but I know it's just how they are, and that doesn't make them any less sad.

"By the way," Mom says. "You might want to put on your Thanksgiving pants. Bela's coming to dinner tonight too.

Paolo makes a fist pump and goes to the cabinet for another plate. This means competition between both Grandma Wong and Abuela Salgado, and we are about to have the best dinner ever.

Mom grabs an onion out of the fridge to dice. All my grandparents at once means plain steamed rice in the rice cooker for Grandma and Papa Wong, and another pot on the stove with onions, garlic, tomato, and chicken bouillon for Paolo and Bela. I'll take a scoop of each to keep things even.

A few minutes later a car pulls into the driveway; then the front door squeaks open. I peek my head around the doorjamb. Sure enough, Grandma Wong's brought enough food to ensure her win against Bela.

Grandma sets down the bags and hugs me, then Paolo. We

each get a cheek pinch, which hurts a little, but I know is as important as the hug. Then she promptly begins arranging all our shoes in neat rows in the entryway.

Papa's holding a platter of Chinese pastries called don tat. They're on Grandma's blue-and-white patterned tray, covered by Saran Wrap. Grandma Wong will never admit it, but we all know she bought them from the Chinese bakery.

I take the platter from Papa and he wraps his arms around me. He has sunflower seeds in his pocket. It's our "spit seeds after dinner and talk" thing. The first time he brought them was after Dad died. Back then, he only brought them when things weren't going well for me. But he brings them more now that I'm in middle school.

Grandma pulls me away from Papa and gives me another hug. "You look like a boy. How is piano?" she asks.

"I stopped piano two years ago, Grandma. Remember? To focus on baseball."

She waves her hand like she can somehow make baseball disappear. "You should play piano . . ." Her facial expression brightens. ". . . or the zither," she says excitedly.

Mom is literally biting her lips together to keep from laughing. "Hi, Cora. Great to see you." Mom helps my grandma with the bags. "You didn't have to bring so much."

I'd normally stick up for my mom, but she was frantically tossing chicken, frozen peas, and some sort of yellow paste in the Crock-Pot before school. Whatever my grandmas bring will be one hundred times better.

143

Grandma Wong sniffs the air. "Save whatever you cooked for you and the kids."

"Yes," Paolo hisses.

My mom glares at him.

Paolo clears his throat. "I meant, I was really looking forward to yellow chicken soup tomorrow night."

Grandma Wong places her dishes strategically in front of where Paolo and I sit, like we'll be the grandma food-off judges. Papa is showing Paolo a trick to make a coin transport through his hand.

Grandma Wong sits in the chair next to mine; that way she can put the food she brought on my plate.

"Lupe, can you run out to the garage and grab a few chairs?" Mom asks, pulling a bowl out of the cupboard.

"Why can't Paolo—"

"Getting a life lesson here." Paolo puts his elbow on the table and rests his chin in his hand, way more interested than he's ever been in one of Papa's tricks. "Fascinating!"

As I pass Paolo on the way out, I mumble, "He's hiding the coin under his thumb."

I turn on the light and go to the opposite side of the garage. The folding chairs are next to Dad's fishing and camping gear. It's also all right next to his baseball bag. His glove sits like a monument right on top of his other belongings.

It's not an ofrenda like Día de los Muertos, but the pile of fishing and baseball gear feels more like Dad than some old picture, some candles, and orange flowers.

And it's more him than the Chinese version of Día de los Muertos, Qingming, where Grandma Wong takes us to the cemetery to burn paper things that represent what she thinks Dad needs in the afterlife. This year she burned a paper house and fake money. I snuck in a paper baseball and bat. When Grandma wasn't watching, I burned them along with a Mariners schedule.

I pick up Dad's glove and oilcloth and sit cross-legged on the garage floor. There's barely any oil left on the scrap of cloth, but I rub the dirt off the leather and polish it using little round circles. When it looks like Dad could pick it up any second to offer a game of catch, I stop. I start to slip my hand in but hesitate. Putting on someone else's glove is pretty personal. You know you're invading their space, because no matter what, it never fits right. Even my own glove needs time and heat and sweat to fit my own hand. Still, I slip it on and close my eyes. I pretend I'm holding his hand.

Then, with it still on my hand, I lay on it like a pillow.

"Lupe," a soft voice calls.

I sit up quickly and set it back in its spot. Grandma Wong walks slowly toward me. "What are you doing?"

How long was she watching? I shrug. "I sort of lost track of time."

For just a second she glances toward the glove. Grandma nods and picks up two folding chairs and hands one to me. We walk inside and she arranges the chairs at the table. I'm grateful she doesn't ask again about how she found me.

Even though Mom told Bela to be there by 6:00 because the

145

plan is to eat at 6:15, it's 6:27 and there's still no sign of her. My mouth waters as I stare at Grandma Wong's steamed eggs.

Grandma Wong nestles in close and rubs her hand over my head while we wait.

Five minutes later, two horn beeps tell us Abuela Salgado is outside. Paolo and I hop up to help her. By the time we approach the front door, Bela tumbles through like a hurricane. She wipes sweat off her brow, and has cornstarch on her cheek. Paolo takes the insulated bag from her hand. She squeezes me even tighter than Papa.

"Párate derecha, Lupe," she says, pushing her finger into my back so my chest goes out. "Deberías estar orgullosa de las chichis. It shows others you are confident." She hands me the flan and grabs my face, kissing me smack on the lips.

Paolo snickers. "She doesn't have those, Bela."

Just what every twelve-year-old wants, her grandma and brother discussing her chest.

Bela narrows her eyes at Paolo and pinches his cheek hard. "What are you talking about? You won't even be able to give me great-grandchildren if you can't keep your room clean."

Paolo tilts his head in confusion.

I cinch my mouth together to keep from laughing, but I'm pretty sure I know where my crappy comeback gene comes from.

"Bela, that doesn't make sense," Paolo says.

"Exactly," she says. "Go clean your room." She kisses him, too, as he tries to wriggle away.

She cups my chin in her hand. "Be proud of what you have, mija."

I look down at my chest. Paolo won that round.

I set the flan down on the counter next to Grandma Wong's impostor don tat, and Bela says hello to everyone and apologizes, complaining about her neighbor's blocking her parking space, then the rain, then traffic, and a pothole.

Bela hurries to wash her hands and sits at the table, while we put her pozole and tamales out. Bela sits on my right side, turning me into a grandma sandwich. Mom reaches out to each side, and we follow her lead all holding hands. Even I see what a diverse mixture of people we are, but sitting together linked like a chain, I feel like nothing can hurt us in our family circle.

"Grace, Paolo," Mom says.

"God, thank you for our grandparents who can cook. No offense," he whispers to Mom.

There's a small knock, followed by, "Ow. And thank you for giving Mr. Montgomery pinkeye so my algebra test is postponed. And help Lupe through puberty and bless this food."

"Paolo," Mom admonishes.

"Oh, sorry," he says, and bows his head again. "Amen."

Mom and Bela sigh simultaneously and cross themselves. Papa and Grandma Wong aren't so religious, but they nod respectfully.

Paolo must be hungry, because he doesn't waste any time spooning pozole into his bowl.

147

Bela smiles and pats his head. "Pozole is magic. It will cure any illness or trouble you have."

"How much do you weigh now?" Grandma Wong asks Paolo.

"Too skinny."

"Yes, too skinny," Bela says in agreement.

Mom sets her chopsticks down. "He's perfect. He just had his physical."

"Mmmmh." Grandma Wong pops a shrimp into her mouth and stares out the window.

Bela ignores Mom's comment and spoons more pozole into Paolo's bowl.

I put a heaping spoon of steamed eggs on top of my white rice and spoon pozole over a scoop of Mexican rice.

I grab the soy sauce, and drizzle barely four drops on top of the eggs.

"Too much soy sauce. Tchhhh," Grandma Wong says.

Paolo narrows his eyes at me just like Grandma, and we erupt in laughter.

"Aiya," Grandma says, shocked at our outburst.

I finish scarfing it all down and stand up with my plate.

"Already done?" Grandma Wong reaches up and pinches my cheek again. "I guess you don't need any more. I can see you've been eating a lot."

Mom drops the shrimp she's holding.

Bela takes my plate from my hand and sets it back down. She takes a tamal from her own plate and sets it on mine. She pulls me back down and I take a bite before she can shovel it into my mouth herself.

I quickly make a muscle with my arm at Grandma Wong. "Gotta keep my strength up, Grandma. Baseball season started."

Bela smiles and pats my knee under the table.

Grandma Wong barely lowers her voice. "No money in baseball. Waste of time."

I slam down *my* chopsticks. It's one thing for her to always call me fat (just a Chinese grandma thing), but it's another to criticize the greatest game in history!

Bela sits up tall and "orugullosas" her "chichis" to show she is confident. "Baseball started in Mexico. It's in her blood," she says.

Paolo snorts into his pozole. Bela's eyes are huge, and her mouth is tight. I sort of appreciate the help. She's dead wrong about its origin of course, but I'm not going to correct her.

Grandma Wong makes a low, "Tchhhh."

There's an eyebrow raising standoff between my grandmas.

Papa is wisely pretending to examine the wood paneling.

I think the only thing my grandmas have in common is forcing Paolo and me to put Vicks VapoRub on our feet and chests if we even hint that we might not feel well.

It gets very quiet.

Bela points to me, and Grandma Wong to Paolo. "Eat more," they say in unison.

I glance at Papa and try to smile, shrugging my shoulders.

Papa Wong folds his napkin, setting it next to his plate, and stands. "Come outside with me, Guadalupe," he says. "There's something I want to show you."

I've never been so grateful for Papa. When we get outside he sits on the back step and pats the ground next to him. I plop down and put my hands on my cheeks. Papa pulls the sunflower seeds out of his pocket and opens the packet.

Something about him opening the seed packet unleashes everything that happened that week. My body slumps even more and I lean into him. Papa puts his arm around my shoulders. "She doesn't always have the best way of saying it, but Grandma wants what she thinks is best for you," he says. "It's just her way."

"You mean it's the *Chinese way*," I say. "She doesn't see who I am at all. Neither of them do. They want me to be *all* of what they are."

"Sometimes people want us to be something we are not, instead of seeing who we really are." His words make me think of square dancing. He cups my hand in his, setting a small pile of seeds in my palm. "You're many things. You are Chinese." He puts a seed in between his lips and shoots a decent six-footer. "You are Latina."

I don't even know if Papa ever heard about how the school expected me to "choose one," and my campaign in the sixth grade to get bubbles like Mexinese or Chinacan added.

"I'm tired of everyone thinking they know what I am . . . or what I should like . . . or what I should do . . ." I toss the seeds into my mouth.

150

"School not going well?" he asks.

Seeds spray from my mouth like an aerosol can.

"Mmmmhhh. I see."

I wipe slobber from my mouth. "I still don't even know what happened. I just didn't want to dance in P.E. But now, everyone hates me, I still have to square dance, and I don't even have a partner. I hate square dancing." I can't really go into the details with Papa about why I want to meet Fu Li so bad. I'd never want him to think I was replacing Dad.

"You know, the energy you put out into the universe is exactly what you get back." Papa makes a slow sweeping motion with his arm in front of him.

I think that might mean he wants me to go with him to tai chi class at the Chinese Senior Center.

"Trying to eliminate an obstacle out of hatred and trying to overcome it after acceptance are two different things. Overcome it instead, Guadalupe."

"But Dad said I should fight for what I want."

"That's true," Papa says.

"I think if Dad had fought harder to keep playing ball, he would've never had to get that last job fishing in Alaska." I'm glad I don't have the sunflower seeds in my mouth. I suddenly have a lump in my throat. "He never would have been on that boat when it went down."

Papa's voice is even softer. "Being a grown-up is complicated. Your father stopped playing baseball for good reasons."

I can't talk. There's no reason good enough. We are way

151

worse off now than if he'd made a lot less money and still been with us.

Papa puts a few more seeds in my hand. "But remember, not all things have to be a fight. Only if there is a good reason," he says. "Accepting something you cannot change and mastering it is not a failure of your principles. It is the opposite of failure."

I'm pretty sure there's no way to make what Papa says and my plan work together. Can I not fight against square dancing but overcome it at the same time?

I blow a seed, and it gets a good two feet on his last spit.

"You're also a strong ball player and powerful girl." He spits another seed a few inches past mine. "You are intelligent . . ." He grabs my chin and looks me in the eye. "But mostly, you are what you believe you are." He sighs and lowers his eyes. "Things I should have told your father when he was your age."

"I'm a good pitcher, Papa."

"I know." He rests his soft brown hand on my cheek. "You *will* pitch in the majors."

I can tell he believes it, and the knot in my throat unravels. None of that helps with my dilemma at school. But knowing I have Papa on my side makes me feel that no matter what happens, I'll be okay.

He stands up and dusts off his pants.

I still have no idea what "accepting something you dislike and mastering it" means exactly. But it sounds like he wants me to accept square dancing and go to the square dancing national finals or start a square dance flash mob.

When we walk back in, Grandma Wong is putting on her opera music, winking at me. "You're going to love this."

I look at Papa, and he covers his smile with his hand and looks away. We sit back down at the table with Mom, Paolo, and Bela.

The plucking of a zither fills the kitchen, and Grandma Wong closes her eyes. She tilts her head back like she's breathing in fresh air. A woman "sings," and her voice is worse than Elmo imitating a whale. *That* is what she thinks is in my blood?

"Isn't it beautiful?" She moves her fingers in front of her like ocean waves.

"Mmmmh," Mom says, not really forming a word.

"She is no Vicente Fernández," Bela says loudly. I cringe, hoping Bela hasn't brought her ranchera music.

The opera singer makes a noise so shrill I bet half the dogs in the neighborhood heard it.

"After this, we can watch the DVD of the Beijing opera I brought," Grandma says. "It's a play called *The Woman Prisoner Su San*."

Bela bends down to reach into her purse, muttering disapproval, and I guarantee Vicente Fernández is tucked somewhere in that big bag.

"Can't!" I blurt out too loudly. I can just imagine the wailing this woman inmate and the old guy in a sombrero can do together.

Everyone stares at me.

I lower my voice. "Homework." I kick Paolo under the table.

153

"Yeah," Paolo chimes in. "Algebra."

Even though it's barely seven, I'm pretty sure Mom's feeling like she's done her daughterly duty for the month. "Grade papers," she mumbles, verifying my suspicions.

Bela makes Paolo eat one more tamal before she leaves so "he's not too skinny to give me grandchildren someday." Papa goes out to start the car. While Mom helps Grandma slip on her coat and collect her bags, I retreat to my room to avoid any further cheek pinching.

"I wanted to say goodbye, Guadalu—" Papa is standing in my doorway, mouth open, eyes wide. "Wait, this is all wrong."

"What? Mom made me clean it. I put my stinky clothes in the wash before you got here."

"Not what I mean." He's already headed toward my bed. "This has to be facing east."

I smack my forehead. I know what's about to happen.

He pushes my bed from right in front of my door where I'd moved it (so I could run and launch into it) to centered against the back wall.

He picks up my cactus plant and sets it in the hall. "Plants grow most at night. *That...*" he points firmly toward where he just evicted my cactus, "... will pull the energy from your sleep." He mumbles something about my "kua number" and within three minutes, Grandma beeping the horn the entire time, my bedroom is fêng shui'd.

"It's not perfect," he says, "but no wonder things have not been going well. Now you will be able to think clearly and things

154

will improve for you." He winks and walks out as Grandma Wong lays on the horn.

Not sure if it was Papa's talk, Bela's pozole, or the fêng shui, but fifteen minutes later, after a rest on my bed, it all suddenly makes sense. I've come up with the only solution that has a chance of working. Why didn't I think of it before? A smiling Fu Li stares at me from his rookie card. Desperate times . . .

I stand up and tighten my ponytail. I open my bedroom door and go across the hall. I stop in front of Paolo's door. "He won't laugh. He won't laugh," I quietly lie to myself.

I knock on the door.

"Entre, peasant," he says. "Better be good. I'm working on something important." Paolo is holding a Mr. Potato Head, who now has Play-Doh boobs and stringy blond hair.

I'm about to ask where he got the hair but decide it might open up conversation on the boobs too. "I need your help," I say.

"Can't. They haven't found the cure for ugly yet."

"I'm serious," I say. "It's important."

"What is it?" He raises one eyebrow and squints the other eye like an evil scientist. "It might cost ya."

A medley of the day's horrors flashes through my mind—smashing into Claire, knocking Gordon down, ruining Samantha's expensive shoes.

"I need you to dance with me."

CHAPTER 16

Paolo sets Skanky Potato Head down. He's completely straight-faced. "I don't dance."

"Please," I beg. "It's square dancing. I need a good grade."

"Oh yeah. Your deal with Uncle Hector to meet Fu Li. Straight As. How funny is it that P.E. is the prob—"

"I know! I know. Will you help me? I need to practice."

Paolo isn't budging. He's never going to go for this.

I turn to leave, then stop in his doorway. "You know, it's sort of your fault."

"How is it my fault?" His voice is higher than usual.

"You could've said something when you had square dancing in seventh grade. I would've had warning. Why would you keep it a secret?"

His face looks like the time Buddy Turner pantsed him in the cafeteria line. And then, I know.

Paolo too has been traumatized by square dancing.

He looks away. "It's . . . it's not important. It was a long time ago." He looks back at me. "What about your partner, the kid who was here the other night? Go force *him* to practice with you."

"Teeeeechnically, Gordon's not my partner."

"Then who is?" he asks.

My stomach is churning again like it was right before P.E. I can't say it out loud.

"Awww, crap. You were the last one standing, weren't you?" He sits on his bed. "That really does suck."

I push a graphic novel over and plop down next to him. "Thanks. That makes it all better."

"It could be worse," Paolo says. "You know who Joey Stewart is?"

I know the kid. He and his sisters all have some rare disease making them outcasts. "The kid with permanent contagious hemorrhoiditis?"

"That's the one," he says. "He didn't have that before square dancing."

"What does that mean? He caught it in P.E.?" I can't even believe what I'm hearing. Square dancing *does* somehow cause diseases!

"What? No!" Paolo puts both hands in front of him for me to calm down. "Just listen. So, on the first day of class when we

157

were supposed to choose a partner, Joey Stewart said all the girls were equally revolting so he'd just take what was left."

"And . . . ?"

"When the music started, we all paired up. Joey was left without a partner, so he started jogging around the gym. He had the ridiculous idea if there was no one to dance with, Coach would let him run laps or clean gum off the bleachers."

I shake my head openmouthed like that's the stupidest idea ever. "Then what?"

Paolo snorts. "Coach told him he had to dance. He argued with her at first. She said she'd fail him right there if he didn't start dancing." Paolo's face breaks into a grin. "Joey started spinning all by himself. He had to walk the circle and go down the dance line alone."

"Yeah, yeah. I know." I motion for him to continue.

Paolo raises his eyebrows. "Then, he bumped into the wrong person."

"I don't get it."

"Joey doesn't actually have permanent contagious hemorrhoiditis."

"What? But . . . but . . . his whole family has it."

"There's no such thing. That rumor was started after he barreled into Sabrina Pinkerton during a square-through maneuver and broke the cell phone hidden in her pocket."

"Samantha Pinkerton's sister?" I slap my hand over my eyes.

"Rumors have a way of spreading," he says. "And with a

ticked-off Sabrina Pinkerton behind the wheel, it was bad." He pats my knee. "See? It coulda been worse."

My mind flashes to Samantha grabbing her foot and squealing like a pig. *These are Pinnacle Stardusts!* echoes in my mind.

This just got way worse than I thought.

But then it dawns on me. If I'm about to have a butt disease, Paolo is too.

"Soooooo . . . Joey's whole family has hemorrhoiditis because of what happened with him and Sabrina?" I click my tongue. "I'm sure Samantha Pinkerton is coming up with something good for me right now after I ruined her fancy shoes today."

Paolo suddenly looks like he has acute anal inflammation already. But there's also something else on his face I haven't figured out yet. He pauses for a few moments.

"Lupe. Out of the kindness of my heart, I won't let that happen to you," he says. "We can fix this. But you'll owe me."

"What's it gonna cost?" I ask.

"We can work out the details later," he says.

I'm desperate for a partner even though Paolo couldn't have been all that great when he had to dance. "Wait. Who was your partner?" I ask.

He cringes like a bee stung him. His face slackens but he doesn't open his eyes.

"Just tell me," I say quietly. I think it's the nicest I've ever spoken to Paolo.

His voice squeaks out, "Sabrina Pinkerton."

"What?! Why would you do that, Paolo?"

He smacks his head over and over like he's trying to knock out the memory. "I was so dumb. As soon as the music started, I just rushed out."

"Oh no."

"I thought if I asked her," he says, "and she *had* to dance with me, she'd get to know me and like me. I might be popular." Paolo falls back onto his bed. "I don't think she even knew who I was."

Now I realize why Paolo ran out of the kitchen like it was on fire when Delia came over for dinner.

"The entire time, my hands were sweaty," he says.

"So? Everyone's hands are sweaty," I say.

"Oh, that's not all." He swallows, then breathes through his nose and out his mouth slowly. "It was right after Dad left to work in Alaska. You remember when Mom went back to work. Crock-Pot leftovers for lunch . . ."

I cringe. "Oh yeah."

"Well, I had P.E. right after lunch."

I remember what fifth grade post-lunch was like. Uncontrollable explosions like an assembly line of champagne corks.

"Oh no."

"Uhhhh . . . yeah. It's hard to hide a fart when you do-si-do and spin around in a mini cyclone for an hour. It wasn't as bad as if I'd broken Sabrina's cell phone like Joey Stewart, but between the hand sweat and farting . . . she told everyone. Sabrina sure knew who I was after that." Paolo stands up and faces me. "It's taken two years for everyone to stop calling me Flutterbutt. I've suffered enough. I can't risk you ruining that for me." He holds his hand out for me.

A weird little sob ekes out and I cover my eyes.

"Awww, crap," he says. "Are you gonna get all emo now?"

I wipe my nose. "No."

"Stand up, Lupe. It's just hormones. They'll go away in a minute."

I grit my teeth. "I don't have those."

He laughs. "Oh yes, you do." He puts his hand on my shoulder. "Listen, I can help you with the dancing part. But the rest . . . Kids can be evil. Teenage girls are especially scary. Just smile and pretend like you're having the best time of your life."

I think of Samantha and Claire, and everyone else plugging their noses at me. I have nothing to lose.

"Joey Stewart . . . and me . . . we let them get in our heads." He taps my forehead. "Don't let them get in yours."

For a split second I think Paolo might actually be okay, but I know I'll probably end up scrubbing the toilet for a year with this deal.

"Let's do this," he says.

I jump to the other side. "Fine. I lead."

CHAPTER 17

A boy walks up to our lunch table on Wednesday and sits down. He must be new. Out of the side of my vision, I can see he has nice clothes and perfect, gelled hair. It's a stark contrast to Niles's jutting-up hair and "Frilled Dogwinkle Snail—Adorable Next Victim of Ocean Warming!" T-shirt, and my loose ponytail and Mariners jersey with a mustard stain down the *I* on the front.

It's not so weird for the new kid to sit at the cafeteria table with the least popular kids. I don't look over. New kid will figure out soon enough about us and find cooler kids to sit with.

"Hey guys," New Kid says.

"Hi," I say. But I don't look up, and continue focusing on dance moves in my mind.

Niles wipes hummus off his mouth. "What's up, Gordon?"

I yank my head toward the new kid. What I'm seeing is very wrong. "Gordon?" I say. "What happened?"

Gordon Schnelly looks like he stepped off the cover of *Tween GQ*. He's wearing dark jeans and an untucked dress shirt. "My grandma's new boyfriend took me out for a guy's day."

"Your hair . . ." I say. Not only is his hair slicked with gel, his goggles are missing.

He rubs his hand over his head, but with all that hair product it doesn't budge. "He took me for a haircut at Julio Marquez Salon and then for *new duds for the new man*," Gordon says in a gravelly voice.

"Do you like it?" Niles asks him.

Gordon shrugs. "I don't know. It feels . . . too . . . polished."

Niles nods and removes a baby carrot from the vegetable bridge he's constructed in his hummus. "Would you rather have a cloak of invisibility, or work as an engineer on the starship *Enterprise*?"

Gordon puts his hand on his chin. Then he unbuttons his fancy new shirt to reveal a glow-in-the-dark *Millennium Falcon* underneath without saying a word. He's still him.

"Starship *Enterprise*, of course. But as you know, if I had my choice, I'd cruise the galaxy in an Imperial Star Destroy—"

"Gordon," I interrupt. "Say 'starship *Enterprise*' again."

He sighs. "Sally sells seashells by the seashore," he says, his lisp completely gone. He makes a fake smile and taps on two perfect front teeth. "Grandma's boyfriend is a maxillofacial specialist, so my prosthetic tooth retainer barely took him an hour."

163

Gordon doesn't look happy about something people normally spend a ton of money on. "I'm having a hard time saying my name."

"You can't say Gordon?" Niles asks.

"No," Gordon says. "Snelly."

"Schnelly," Niles corrects.

"I know." Gordon crumples up his napkin. "I can't say it anymore. It's these new teeth."

"I liked you better the other way," Niles says, pulling out his apple juice.

"Shhhhh." I tap Niles under the table.

"You did?" Gordon asks Niles.

"Yeah. It's who you are." Niles takes a long drink from his juice box, then says quietly, "Nature doesn't make mistakes."

By the smile on Gordon's face, Niles just undid enough damage in those ten seconds that would've taken years of counseling with Delia.

***

It's been five days and Andy is still giving me the cold shoulder. There's no time to fix our friendship before I go out to overcome square dancing. Instead, I run to the sink, wet down my hair, and tighten my ponytail. I've worn spandex, so today my shorts won't ride. I even shaved my legs and the two hairs on my armpit. I am ready.

I hold my chin high and walk into the gym. Gordon (a.k.a.

Excessive-Science-Goggle Wearer) has the nerve to arch his eyebrows at the sweatbands on my wrists.

We pair up, and I'm with Gordon and Zola, Andy and Niles, and two other kids. When Zola sees Gordon, her face looks like she just got asked to prom by the quarterback of the football team. "H-h-hi, Gordon." Even though he has on his regular old dorky gym shorts, he still looks different with product in his hair and a complete mouth of teeth.

The music starts almost instantly so we don't have to listen to Zola falling all over the new Gordon.

I step on Andy's foot once. She doesn't react at all.

The caller wails out, "Back to your partners!"

We switch and I'm alone again. We promenade, and I bump into Niles.

"Sorry, dude."

Niles nods and keeps moving. He and Andy aren't making any mistakes. There's a twinge in my stomach. I watch them too long and miss a do-si-do.

I'm losing focus. I spin with just enough room and come back to my position.

But when I put my hand out to link into Andy's for an allemande left, I completely miss and trip over my feet. I switch to my invisible partner. If I can't have a real partner, I need to visualize I'm with Paolo. I swipe my forehead with my wristband.

I stop and close my eyes. Paolo and I are spinning arm in arm. We switch to the other direction and lock hands in perfect form.

When I open my eyes, Coach is staring at me.

I give her a thumbs-up. She's far away, but I think I see a thumb peek out from behind her clipboard.

We switch to the next group. Samantha's eyes shift up and to the right when we make eye contact. I'm sure it means she's trying to figure out some fake disease for me. Instead, she grunts and flings Blake's hands off her when he promenades in the wrong direction, nailing her in the calf.

"You're horrible!" Samantha shrieks. She stops in the middle of the circle and faces him. The rest of us keep clapping with the music and avoid eye contact. "Any professional could see you have zero command of rhythm. You're about as coordinated as the wacky waving tube man at my dad's car dealership. Even Lupe's better than you."

For a split second, I think she deserves another Silent But Deadly bombing mission the next time she's my partner. But it's also about the nicest thing she's ever said about me.

Blake starts up the routine again, spinning her a little too fast. "Well, you're dumb . . . and . . . and you smell like you slept in rotten fruit."

"It's Shower Factory's Pea Blossom, you caveman," she says.

Banjos drown out her voice. "Switch partners."

Blake looks relieved, but now I'm on the receiving end of Samantha's stink-eye.

"Half sashay."

Samantha and I move in an arc around each other. Paolo said

to smile and pretend I'm having fun. I smile as big as I can and rock my head from side to side at her the entire time.

Samantha pulls her entire upper body away. "Stop that! It's creepy."

I keep smiling. If she's going to give me a disease, I'd rather it be something about how I'm a few McNuggets short of a Happy Meal.

We move to the next partner. I do the same to Claire. She flinches back, and her mouth is open. I double-time my head-rocking.

Then I'm back with Samantha. I grin and keep bobbing my head.

"You're such a freak." Samantha stumbles over her feet. "If you don't stop, I'll tell Coach Solden you're smiling at me."

I smile even bigger, then bow.

"Back to your partners!" the caller says.

I'm back with an invisible Paolo. I do-si-do, then do-pas-so. I'm no flourisher, but I'm catching on. I bet I could even keep up with Gordon.

Coach is walking around the perimeter of the court. Her clipboard is resting on her hip, and she scribbles marks on a sheet as she watches us. I smile and wave at her.

The bell rings, ending class. Coach shakes her head and smiles.

CHAPTER 18

At baseball practice all through the next week, the pocket radar clocks me at sixty-five miles an hour, so suddenly Blake is running to the mound every so often like *he* is the one responsible for my new record speed.

By the end of practice Thursday, Marcus is the only one ignoring me because his mom decided every Sunday was going to be cornbread-casserole-and-square-dancing night at their house.

By Friday, spandex secure under my gym shorts, I don't bump into a single person during P.E. I nail every spin and do-si-do and do-pas-so without even a passing foot stomp. Exactly like Papa Wong said, overcoming worked better than fighting.

I arrive home from school to an empty house. It wasn't such a bad day, but I have no baseball practice, no homework . . . and no Andy.

But, I still have Niles. I realize it's technically the weekend, so after dinner I decide to check in on his *Doctor Who* weekend-marathon idea. I hop on my bike and I'm at his front door in less than a minute.

His mom answers the door. "Hi, Lupe. How are things going?"

I catch a strange whiff of vanilla and what I think is rosemary. "Oh, great!" I say, inching away so she can't pull me into her laboratory and douse me with *Confidence* or *Success*.

"They're in Niles's room," she says, like I should know who she's talking about.

They?

She motions with her eyes down the hall.

The ping in my stomach is back full force, and now it's a resounding gong. Whatever or whoever *they* are, I'm probably about to find out why Niles has been bailing on our Monday night *Doctor Who* dates. I debate asking Mrs. Foster if she has an oil called *Don't Panic*.

I walk down the hallway and hear voices.

I hesitate at his door.

I make my signature knock, tap, tap, knock.

"Come in, Lupe."

I open the door, and Gordon and Niles are sitting on flat, square pillows. Soft music eerily similar to Grandma Wong's Chinese opera music plays in the background. Niles is seated cross-legged. He's spinning his Post-it note pen in one hand without even looking. Gordon is sitting across from him. Part of Niles's

169

Doctor Who nebula poster is now covered by a *Star Trek* poster with three very serious faces emerging from a rainbow.

I glance around. Bruce Lee is still on the wall and Niles's martial arts stuff is on the chair as always.

His red graphic novel skyscraper is two stories higher than the last time I was here.

Gordon's still wearing his fancy new clothes. His hair has just as much product in it, but he's wearing earmuffs that are brown cinnamon-bun spirals like General Organa had when she was young and wore dresses. He has a pink "Superstar!" Post-it on his forehead. They have models of spaceships arranged between them in orderly rows. This visit might not have been the best idea.

I keep my distance at the door, afraid I might be sucked into this new vortex, but also wondering what's going on with Niles. "Gordon. Hi. I didn't expect to find you here. What are you up to?"

I guess I should be happy we are all becoming friends. It's not like they're excluding me right now. So why am I jealous?

"Just men talking shop," Gordon answers.

"Spaceships?" I ask.

I can't help but notice, once again, that Niles has traded in his *Doctor Who* PJs for some covered with the words "Live Long and Prosper" and "Where No Man Has Gone Before." My stomach suddenly feels like I never ate dinner at all.

Niles waves his hand without the spinning pen for me to come in. "Actually, we'd taken a break to discuss baseball."

This *was* a good idea. I close the door and plop down between them. "Can you believe the Mariners traded—"

Gordon laughs and nudges Niles. "We were talking about pitching, Lupe."

"Oh. Well. If that's the case, I'm happy to answer any questions," I say.

Gordon sighs. "Physics. We were talking about the physics of a knuckleball."

I glance at Niles. "Huh?"

Niles faces me, setting his pen down. "Actually, Gordon was talking physics. The goal of a knuckleball is to give the ball as little rotational spin as possible, right?"

I nod.

"You know," Gordon says. "The pitch's path shifts from the difference in the smooth surfaces of the ball in contrast to its rougher seams."

I actually don't know. I shrug my shoulders. "Okay?" This is where most people would leave me behind. But not Niles. True to form . . .

"People argue about why it flutters around," Niles adds. "I say not everything's meant to be measured. It's probably a combination of things, and it probably depends on the form of the pitcher."

Gordon leans in toward Niles. "You can't ignore air flow or the theory that seams are what create the zigzag pattern and lift."

Although I've never been able to throw one, and it's like my holy grail, I don't think I'll ever understand how the knuckleball actually works. I look back and forth between them. I have nothing to add.

"Niles insists that I'm applying too much science, and that sometimes a pitcher just has the 'feel' of something." He rolls his eyes, making air quotes. Gordon puts his hand on Niles's shoulder. "I believe we are at an impasse, my friend."

I realize the two of them might have things in common that I can't be part of. I should be happy about this.

Niles glances at me, and I can't help the frown and shoulder slump. He turns to Gordon. "Wanna discuss the knuckleball another time?"

"Sure," Gordon says. "How about we chat about how the *Millennium Falcon* would kick the *Enterprise*'s butt in an intergalactic skirmish?"

The corner of Niles's mouth turns up ever so slightly. "It'd never happen," he says. "Your ship sacrifices control for hyperdrive propulsion."

Gordon's eyebrow arches. "You've just made my point, comrade. The *Falcon* can evade attacks using its speed."

"But the *Enterprise* can maneuver at high warp. The *Millennium Falcon* is fast but ineffective in close combat." Niles picks his pen back up and within a second it's a whirring blur again. "So you'd run from galactic conflict versus facing battle?"

"How about the TARDIS?" I say, trying to chime in.

They both shift their gaze to me simultaneously. I think I might be out of my league on this one.

"I mean, she has a soul," I continue, "and she can just dematerialize in one spot then rematerialize—"

Gordon snorts. "Not really in the same galaxy, Lupe. No offense."

I sigh and fold my hands in my lap.

They continue, talking about ships that warp and shoot and go to battle, nothing like the Doctor's.

Enough is enough. Seeing how much fun they're having together, and how out-of-place I'm feeling, just makes me miss Andy even more. I can't take another day without her.

"Hey. I think I'm going to take off, guys."

They're so into it, they barely notice as I scoot out the door. I glance back and smile, knowing this is a good thing. I need to accept Niles making new friends and find a way to patch things up with Andy.

I get on my bike and speed toward Andy's house. I'll have her back as my best friend and be home before my mom gets off work, so I can ask if Andy can sleep over.

I round the corner to her house so fast, my tires almost skid out from under me. Andy's home comes into view. A group of kids are running behind bushes and cars avoiding water balloons. Andy ducks behind a trash can, barely dodging a bright red balloon . . . but that can't be her. Even though I love them, Andy hates water balloon fights.

I recognize the other girls running around screaming and laughing as the soccer kids.

I leave my bike across the street and walk over to her. "Hey, Andy."

She turns around. Her mouth drops open. "What are you doing here?"

I smile, but not the creepy smile I made in P.E. "Can I talk to you?"

She looks over her shoulder back at the girls who've all stopped hurling balloons and are staring at us. "I'm sorta busy," she says, holding out a green water-filled balloon.

Jordyn walks over and stands next to her like they're some sort of team now. Neither of them is smiling back. My stomach sinks, wondering if Andy might've already shared New Yack with Jordyn.

"I just wanted to see if we could talk," I say.

Jordyn tugs at Andy's arm. "We don't need any more players. Do we, Andy?"

Andy takes a few steps backward. "You should go."

I can't believe this is happening. No matter what, I could always count on Andy. "But you hate water balloons."

"No, I don't. My new friends don't yell 'butt-burner' and aim for my—" Andy stops and closes her eyes. "Just leave, Lupe."

We were nine! You're supposed to—Why didn't she tell me she hated balloon butt-burners?

"Andy, I . . . I'm . . . sorry. About everything." I have to make this better, but she's not letting me. My chin is starting to tremble. "Can I come over later and talk to you alone?"

"I have plans," Andy says.

"Wow, someone can't take a hint." Jordyn turns and walks back toward the other girls.

Andy lets out an annoyed breath and puts one hand on her hip. "Besides, like you said, I'm a *joiner*. Right?" Andy lets the balloon slip out of her fingers like it's some sort of symbolic mic drop, and it explodes on the ground. She follows Jordyn without giving me the chance to say anything else.

For a second, I just stand there. How can you be best friends with someone for six years and they replace you with more popular kids in less than a week? Mom has always said I only needed one good friend to survive . . .

It's my fault she's walking away. Figuring out how much I've messed up might've come too late.

The thought of middle school without Andy is terrifying.

I have no one.

I cross the street and pick up my bike, snickers following me. I put on my helmet and pedal home as fast as I can. My legs are shaking. The bike wobbles beneath me, but I keep pedaling. Tears roll down my cheeks and into my chinstrap.

***

I really do think it helped when Papa Wong did his fêng shui thing to my room, but right now it isn't working. I've been lying on my bed for twenty minutes and I still have never felt so horrible. I can't very well put my cheek on Dad's picture in the hallway with everyone home. So I do the next best thing. I pull Fu Li's rookie card off the wall and put it against my cheek. Just for a second, I pretend it's Dad. I even think I smell coffee.

175

Someone knocks on my door and I cram the card inside my pillowcase. I pretend to be asleep but right when they open the door, I do that uncontrollable breathing thing that sounds like I'm stuttering my breath in.

Mom is already rushing to my side. "Oh no. What happened?"

Now I'm really blubbering. *Everyone hates me* comes out as "E . . . ev . . . y. . . . hay . . . me."

My mom interprets ugly-cry language really well. "No they don't." She wipes my tears with the sleeve of her sweater. "What happened?"

"An . . . di . . . ha new frei."

"Well, I bet you can be friends with them too. Let's invite them all over."

It's been too long since my mom was in middle school. I'm pretty sure they didn't have cliques back when she was my age.

It's a fine line. I can't tell my mom Andy won't even talk to me. She might do that protective-mom thing and stay mad at her, or worse . . . call Andy's mom. So instead, I give her a look like she's lost her mind with her suggestion.

"Not . . . how . . . works . . . ma . . ."

She tucks a loose hair behind my ear. "Do you want to tell me what happened? Surely Andy didn't just abandon you."

My fight with Andy echoes in my mind. *Your mom can pull strings.* Then. *Peed your pants.* Then. *Jockstrap.* Then. *You can't even stand up to your mom.*

I really can't tell my mom.

Worry lines crease her forehead. I need to pull it together.

176

I force a smile and take a minute to get my breathing back to normal. In that moment I come to a decision. Even if Andy never talks to me again, I have to try to listen to people more instead of worrying about myself and my own goals.

Mom rubs my hair plastered with tears and snot off my face. "I logged on to the school portal while you were gone. You are having a good quarter aren't you? As in almost everything? That's good news, right?" She leans in and kisses my cheek. "A little more work and you'll have your straight As to meet Fu Li."

Another downside to a parent who's also a teacher, besides having your teachers as built-in baby monitors: teacher-parents actually check on your grades. *Sniff.* "Sure . . . I guess P.E. is the only class still up in the air."

My mom walks toward the hall but winks to me as she leaves. "Well, I think I've got something to cheer you up. Coach Solden's going to reveal the top square dancers for the Salmon Days assembly next week!"

CHAPTER 19

I haven't had enough time! It's been barely two weeks to convince Coach I'm good enough. And I only had one good dancing day. Now I only have one more chance. I know there were at least four teams about the same or better than me in class. If I can be in perfect form Monday during P.E., I might just make the cut by the time she announces the winners at the end of class.

I jump out of bed and pull Fu Li's card out of the pillowcase and hang it back on the wall. "You want straight As. You got it!"

I run to Paolo's room and pound on his door.

"What!"

His door flies open and this time he's wearing a yellow-and-orange luchador mask and holding Legos in the shape of Smurfette.

"What is . . ." I point my finger at his covered face, then Smurfette, then decide not to even ask.

"What do you want, cretin?" he says.

"Can you dance with me for a little bit?"

He goes to slam his door and I lean against it. "We had a deal." I push harder, but my feet are slipping backward as the door shuts.

He grunts. "I'm not your servant boy, Lupe."

"Only for a little bit!" I push harder. "I'll clean your room." I can't believe I just said that to someone who thinks clean underwear means you hang dirty ones on your doorknob to air out overnight. I'll have to touch boogers and God knows what else. And I don't have a hazmat suit.

The door swings open and I fly inside and onto a pile of disgust. I gag and cough, then jump up from the mound of clothes that smell like a wet dog stuffed in the back of a closet for a year. "What the—" I say.

He pulls off the mask and tosses it in the pile. "Aaaaand . . . you just agreed to clean that up. You've got thirty minutes of my time tomorrow. But only after I finish my important project." He sets the Lego Smurfette gently on his desk.

He pushes me out the door. I fight back one last time, shoving against it just to be difficult. "Fine." I let go and the door slams. I hope the thump I hear is Paolo's head.

I grab my *Doctor Who* TARDIS robe off the hook on my door and wrap it around me. I wish it was a real time-and-space

179

machine and I could be the Doctor's companion. I could fly off to Gallifrey and make this all go away.

When I curl up next to Mom on the couch, she pulls me under her arm. "Feeling better, little one?"

"I guess," I say.

"Give me a minute." She stands and goes to the kitchen, and I hear a pot clank. A few minutes later, the smell of popcorn fills the house.

She walks back in with a huge plastic bowl. "I've got just the thing." She grabs the remote and pulls up season four. But instead, all I can think of is how I saw these episodes first with Niles.

Mom rubs the hair out of my face. "I love you to the Moon of Poosh and back, mija."

Rose has always been the best match for the Doctor to me. They feel like home, so with Mom rubbing my head, and *Doctor Who* playing, I'm asleep before they step out of the TARDIS.

When I wake up, I'm on the couch with sun in my eyes, a blanket tucked around me, and popcorn in my hair.

Paolo's still asleep, so I practice dancing by myself for a while.

An hour later, Paolo's still not up, so I go outside to pitch my eighty-one in the zone. I warm up with ten straight fast pitches, then a few changeups. I throw a curveball and hit the edge of the pocket, barely making it in.

I need to focus. If I can nail these tougher pitches, I can nail the dancing thing.

My dad's voice comes in like a calming breeze. *Listen, Cute Toot.*

Guilty, but not exactly what a great pitcher wants as a

180

nickname. *Now pitching, Cute Toot—Luuuuupe Woooooong!* To prove my maturity, I pitch a few circle changes and four seamers—all in the zone. I feel like I can conquer almost anything.

By the time you're in high school, if you work hard enough, you'll throw a knuckleball, Dad says. *You keep at it and you've got a chance to make it to the show.*

I've tried a thousand times before. If only I could throw a real one . . .

My hands are still too small to get my knuckles on the seam. I think about what Niles said. Maybe it's not all science. Maybe each pitcher just has to find their own "feel" for it. I grip my fingernails along the seam and slip my thumb to the underside.

Remember, if it's more than one rotation, it doesn't count, Dad says.

I dig in with my toe to steady myself.

I imagine my dad demonstrating for me, thrusting one arm out. *You gotta throw and push.*

I step forward just like him and push. The ball dances a little back and forth, then hits directly in the center of the pitching square with a deep thunk.

It's only one, but I did it! My glove falls from my hand.

If I can perfect the knuckleball, I can for sure make it in the majors. And if I can pitch a knuckler, I can square dance.

I run to Paolo's room and pound on his door. "Paolo! Get. Up."

Crashing echoes from inside his room. "I said sometime tomorrow. Not the butt crack of dawn," he yells.

I open his door. "It's eleven." Liquid from a tipped-over water glass and scattered Cheetos melt into his carpet.

181

He clamps his pillow over his head. "Okay, Okay."

The first few rounds, we have some random bumps and trips, but the next seven are near perfect. By the time we finish, I'm way more polished than I was on Friday.

Paolo finishes with a brotherly push, launching me onto the couch. "Now don't bug me unless you come prepared with food offerings," he says, disappearing back to his room.

When Coach sees on Monday how good I am now, I *will* have my A in P.E. Cinching the 4.0 I need to meet Fu Li, since the rest of my classes have been going great. Between throwing a knuckle-ball and square dancing with the worst possible partner, nothing can defeat me!

I decide to close the deal and wind down a little by practicing on my own. I type in "Turkey in the Straw song." Barney the Dinosaur tops the list. Even if he hadn't been wearing a cowboy hat and boots, I have a strict anti-Barney policy. He's followed by an NPR report, "The Ice Cream Song—Origins Are Not What You Think!" I really don't have time to be reading old-people news, but I click on it knowing it'll at least have the song.

Instead of the music I'm hoping for, a lady with curly blond hair and thick black glasses speaks with a British accent. "For decades, Americans have celebrated with the tradition of square dancing. The majority of these songs got their beginnings in the South."

No mystery. Andy and I saw how lots of the songs were originally sung by enslaved people.

"But what many of you don't know, is that most of these songs have altered versions steeped in racism." She stops and stares at me. Well, not me, but the camera.

"Columbia Gramophone Records released a version in 1916 that is so disturbing . . ." Her voice actually trembles a little. ". . . I will just let the song speak for itself."

The familiar ice cream truck song begins. The music is crackly. But just like with the version I'm used to, a man with a Southern accent yells out.

The N-word rolls off the singer's tongue like he is used to saying it all the time. He calls out in a mocking voice for "them" to come have ice cream, then sings over and over again that N loves a watermelon. Did kids like me have to dance to these words at some point? This is the heritage they want us to celebrate? My stomach kneads slowly like I ate rotten meat.

All I can think of is how Andy would feel if she were here. Tears sting my eyes. This isn't that same thing as throwing my jacket over some pee puddle to protect her.

Even though she wants nothing to do with me, I can never let her hear that song.

CHAPTER 20

The sky is dark and the rain is coming down in sheets. The school corridors are especially dangerous in this kind of weather. Instead of going to the cafeteria for lunch with Niles and Gordon, I walk toward Principal Singh's office.

I've spent the entire morning in class wondering if I'm doing the right thing. I was so close to my A and meeting Fu Li—who knows what'll happen now. I huddle into a corner by my locker to think this through. If I just stay right here and never tell anyone, they might never find out. And once I walk through Principal Singh's doors, I might be making this all worse. I could be drawing attention to that version of the song. Andy might hear the horrible words and it would be because of me.

But if I do nothing, the song is still out there. And if someone hears it, and thinks that others know about it and didn't say anything, what will they think?

I can't know what it would feel like for Andy to hear that song, but I know what it feels like to hurt. And when you see bad stuff in the world, you have to speak up. Even if Andy's still mad at me ten years from now for what I said to her, when she hears that song, maybe she'll at least know I tried to do the right thing.

Meeting Fu Li will have to take a back seat.

This is one of those days you don't go into the salmon run of students unless you're ready to do battle. I pull my backpack tight and step out from the shadows. I walk straight down the center of the hallway toward Principal Singh's office.

Papa's words about how I didn't always have to fight against things, unless there's a good reason? I can't think of a better one.

I have nothing prepared. No PowerPoint presentation. No bullet points. Just those awful words echoing in my mind. I don't know how I'll ever hear that tune again and be able to think of anything different.

I knock on her door and wait.

"Yes?"

I open the door and stand square in the middle of the door-frame. Principal Singh is sitting crisscross-applesauce on a yoga mat on the floor.

"Can this wait, Miss Wong?"

Just like the lady on NPR, I can't keep my voice from shaking. "It's pretty serious."

185

She rolls up her yoga mat, mumbling, "Guess it's a good time. Any other time, I might not be so calm." She takes a long drink from her water bottle, standing up. "So, what can I help you with?"

I catch myself picking my nail like Andy. "I saw something in a news report. Something bad. And I'm not sure how to tell you about it."

"Well, can you show me what you saw?" she asks, sitting at her desk.

She looks a little surprised when I walk around the side of her desk and lean over her to type on her keyboard. I type in the same search from the night before. Sure enough, Barney pops up. Right below him is the NPR report.

"What's this?" she says.

I click on the link. The English woman begins speaking about the origins of square dancing.

Principal Singh suddenly doesn't sound so calm. "Lupe, if this is about getting the song changed again—"

"Just listen." I tap on the keyboard, turning up the volume. Right there in Principal Singh's office the ice cream truck song starts up.

The crackled words on the old record get louder. Principal Singh's eyes skim back and forth as she reads the article along with the report. She's not smiling.

After the second verse, she hits mute. "I've heard enough." It's silent except for the ticking of a small clock on her desk. I think this is one of those times I need to just shut up and wait.

186

She looks away, speaking softly. "I did then what I knew how to do. Now that I know better, I do better."

I'm not sure if she's talking to me or to herself. Still, they're super smart words.

She finally turns to face me and puts a hand on my shoulder. "I need to think about how exactly I'm going to handle this, but you did the right thing calling this to my attention."

"Principal Singh, you do know though that if you change the song again, I may as well transfer to Antarctic Middle School now."

"This isn't about the entire song," she says.

Did she not hear those words?

"Lupe, square dancing isn't disgusting. The tune isn't disgusting. The lyrics someone made up are disgusting."

"But someone made them that way," I say.

"And we don't have to accept it."

I see her point, but something still doesn't sit right. I just can't put my finger on it. "Principal Singh. I don't want you to think I'm complaining about square dancing . . ."

Her eyebrows peak so high they nearly hit her hairline.

". . . but I don't get why we all have to do it," I say. I think of the lion dance at the Chinese New Year's parade. The pounding drums vibrating my chest. Feeling like I want to jump and fly over the ground just like the lions. Watching Bela dance the jarabe tapatío, twirling her imaginary skirt. "I mean, I'm American, and I'm not seeing how square dancing relates to me or my background. I've never seen anyone in my family or any of my friends square dancing before P.E. Does your family square dance?"

187

Principal Singh laughs. "No."

"So, why is everyone ignoring that *this* dance leaves most of us out?"

Is eliminating it what I even want anymore? I've finally conquered it. I could've actually been one of the finalists. This is what it feels like to be torn between finally getting what I want and knowing something doesn't feel right.

She smiles. "You're right, Lupe. But, square dancing isn't bad; it's just—" The bell to go to fifth period rings, interrupting her. "I can't help you unhear those words, so you'll have to give me a chance to find a way to replace them for you."

"How can someone replace something like that?" I ask.

She taps her finger on her desk. "Look at what Julius Lester and Jerry Pinkney did for books. Little Black Sambo and the Uncle Remus stories were full of racist content. Yet, they took those stories and reinvented them to create something cherished and beautiful for their community, for all of us. We can do the same."

"So, we're still . . ."

"Oh, yes," she says standing. "Since 1938, the Issaquah Middle School Sockeyes—"

"I know." I sigh and walk toward the door.

This means we're still square dancing, and I still need to be one of the finalists.

All I can think of is how I'm going to get the blame for whatever new policy Principal Singh comes up with. "Can you not tell anyone who told you?"

She laughs and follows me to the door. "I think somehow people will know." She gives me a hug. "But of all your causes, this is one you should be extremely proud of. I'm glad you came to me. And I think I just thought of a way to make Issaquah Salmon Days even better, to start."

I have no idea what she could be up to, but with my track record (and even though it was the right thing to do), I'm pretty sure I've just pounded the last nail in my social coffin.

CHAPTER 21

Gordon and Niles are waiting to go to fifth period by my locker. They are rock-paper-scissoring over something. Each time, they finish with laughter, and I wonder if they're doing it just for fun. This is not the right time to tell them what just happened with Principal Singh.

"Come on guys."

It's like someone released fifty roller-derby teams onto a greased track. Gordon, Niles, and I stick close together. Our combined body mass lessens the chance of one of us getting launched off the path and into the mud.

Coach Solden passes alongside us.

"Hey Coach," I say.

She nods at us and fumbles her keys, looking quickly away.

Gordon is so close that the unevenness in his voice is even

more loud and unsettling. "What do you make of that?" he says, motioning to Coach. Being a finalist is as important to Gordon as it is to me, but for entirely different reasons.

Unless they have earpieces, Coach couldn't know about my conversation with Principal Singh yet.

I pat him on the shoulder. "Maybe she's in a hurry, or maybe she just doesn't want to play favorites." I'm not sure if I'm trying to make Gordon feel better or myself. "Listen, we have one last chance to convince her. Just make sure we're in the same group so everyone else suffers by comparison." We stop in between a section of lockers and out of the way of danger.

"I have to have my game face on today," Gordon says. "The man is back." He takes off his backpack and gives it to Niles. He runs his hands back and forth vigorously through his hair, messing up any gel-comb-job. It's not as frizzy and wonky as it used to be, but it's a close second. He slips off his new designer Hike-Tech fleece jacket. It gets stuck on his arms so I help pull him out of it. Underneath, on his T-shirt, Yoda leans on a walking stick, eyes narrowed. "There Is No Try . . ." is written across the top.

Gordon drifts a bit and just stands there, staring at all the people passing. He's too far out into the traffic path and gets bumped hard.

"Careful," I pull Gordon back closer to the wall. "Are you crazy? Let's get to P.E. We go on three." I hold his fleece out for him to take. Niles takes it instead and drapes it over Gordon's backpack.

Gordon's voice is shaky. "There's something I need to do

first." He reaches up and unclips his prosthetic teeth retainer. Underneath is the gap from Gordon's missing front tooth, and his chipped other front tooth. It makes me smile. I missed his old teeth. But when I shift my gaze to Gordon's eyes, something in his stare makes my blood freeze. He's taking deep breaths and staring down at the teeth his grandma's boyfriend made him. His face looks paler than a minute ago.

"What's wrong, Gordon?" I ask.

"The old me was better," he says. "I shouldn't change just so people will like me."

Niles smiles at him. "If you're the real you, the right people will love you."

Is there something I'm missing here?

Gordon closes his eyes tight and throws his fake teeth into the river of kids. He stares out at them but doesn't move until they've been trampled on. Then, he steps out after them.

I yell out. "Gordon! Noooooo!"

Niles locks his elbow through mine before I can plunge in after him.

"Let him go," Niles says.

It's too late anyway. Gordon is five feet downstream, and with the number of kids between us, it may as well be a mile. Instead of following the code and staying upright so he doesn't get decapitated, he kneels down for the teeth. His big head is an easy target. His body flails around as he takes a trombone case to the face and a backpack to the gut. By the time he's still, he's ten feet away, off the cement path and into the mud. He pushes himself

192

up and stands. Blood is dripping out of his nose. One eye is closed.

He's holding the mangled retainer between his fingers up in the air like it's a prize.

***

I nearly lose a shoe helping Gordon out of the mud. His nose stops bleeding quickly. Besides a crust of dark red under Gordon's nose, there's no evidence of his sabotage of the expensive tooth repair. But his eyelid is definitely swollen shut.

Niles doesn't seem to be surprised by any of this. I wonder how much of that the two of them planned out in advance.

"Did you really have to throw your teeth out there?" I ask. "You couldn't have just stomped on them in the safety of the classroom?"

His lisp is back in full force. "Now it won't be a lie when I tell my grandma I needed to go after my new teeth. It was the right decision. Right?" He makes an exaggerated wink. "Schnelly . . . Schnelly . . ." he says, like he's performing a sound check. He smiles a huge gap-toothed grin. "I feel a lot more like myself now." He takes a deep breath and marches confidently toward P.E.

We turn the corner and the gym comes into view. My stomach does a flip. I'm sure Gordon is in prime position to be a finalist, but the next hour is do-or-die time for me. I look at Gordon's shirt and notice Yoda has a fresh blood drop on the point of his hairy ear. This is one of those times I need to put friends

193

first. And even though my life depends on not being tardy today . . .

"Don't you think we should go to the nurse?" I ask him.

"No way," Gordon says. "I've been waiting two weeks for this moment."

I pull a Kleenex from my backpack and run it under a drinking fountain. "Hold on, Gordon." I wipe it under his nose, removing any evidence that might get him sent home.

Gordon and Niles disappear into the boys' locker room. Niles waves back at me over his head.

When I walk in the girls' side, Andy is already at our lockers, facing me.

She glances down. I follow her eyes to where she's staring. Mud is all over the tiles in a shoe-print path from where I just walked in. My shoes and socks are like chocolate-dipped marshmallows from helping Gordon out of the mud pit.

Muddy footprints in Coach's gym will for sure get me marked down. I take them off and hurry to the sink. I turn the faucet to full blast and scrub them with a paper towel. After a minute they're no longer brown, but they're dripping. I turn on the hand dryer, but Coach blows her whistle and I'm out of time. I barely have a second to throw on my gym clothes and make it out before class starts.

I run out and stand next to Gordon and Zola so I can be in their group.

Zola gasps at Gordon. "What happened? Your teeth . . . your hair . . ."

Gordon bites his lip with his snaggletooth. One eye is half-closed.

Zola is not very concerned about what is obviously going to be one heck of a shiner.

"I think he looks great," I say.

Gordon smiles and his cheeks get blotchy.

Zola squints and tilts her head a tiny bit like that will somehow transform him back to *GQ* Gordon with perfect hair and teeth.

Gordon turns away from her, facing the center of our square. "I appreciate your concern, Zola. I, for one, am quite pleased with my more recent makeover, which I handled myself."

Coach blows her whistle. "Listen up. I'm sure you are all on pins and needles to see who's going to represent your gym class in the Salmon Days assembly. So, without further ado, here are the winners!"

This can't be right. She has to see how much better I am! I jump out of our dance circle and raise my hand, waving it around.

Coach isn't looking up from her clipboard. "The first couple—" she says.

"Waaaaaait!" It comes out way louder than I meant it to.

Everyone turns to look at me. Coach glares up from her paper. She tilts her head. "This better be good."

"Aren't we going to dance first?" I rock back and forth on mushy feet. The sloshing echoes in the gym.

Coach's chin drops to her chest and she closes her eyes like she can't take one more minute of this nonsense.

195

I try to put my hands in pockets that aren't there. "You know . . . so you can fully assess our progress."

"Yeah," Gordon makes an overexaggerated palm-up appeal in front of him like he's pleading for his life. "We lost a scheduled day of dancing because of Capture the Flag."

Someone coughs out, "Morons."

"Marcus, come see me after class," Coach says without even looking up from her clipboard. She tucks her clipboard under her arm and pinches the bridge of her nose with her fingers. "I'm making my announcement first, then we can dance. You two can stay after school too and dance all you want since you love it so much. I'm happy to provide the music."

"Touché, Coach Solden," Gordon whispers. "Maybe we just will."

I clench soggy socks between my toes. What's done is done. All of it was for nothing. I look around and find Andy. I know she can see me, but she doesn't look back.

"Ahem. The first couple I hope can work a little harder and pull it together before Friday." Coach peeks out from behind her clipboard. "Samantha and Blake."

A few sporadic claps come from people who aren't sure how we're supposed to react to the winners. But mostly it's awkward silence.

Samantha and Blake were a given. Samantha could dance with an elephant and still be a finalist.

Blake smiles at Samantha, and she makes her signature

flutter-eye-roll that looks more like she's having some sort of seizure.

"For best teamwork—" Coach stares up and down the line, one side of her mouth turned up higher than the other. She raises an eyebrow. "Niles and Andalusia."

Niles's eyes go as wide as jumbo eggs, and Andy makes a noise sounding oddly like, "Meep."

Andy smiles at Jordyn, but I can't help but notice Jordyn doesn't smile back. Andy and Niles turn to face each other. "You did it!" they say at the same time. "Jinx!" they yell, then laugh.

Gordon pats Niles's shoulder. "Good job, buddy." But Gordon's voice doesn't have its normal enthusiasm.

Kids are mumbling but I think it has more to do with what they are going to do after school than who won the square dancing competition. I'm pretty sure Gordon and I are the only ones who care about who will be announced next.

Coach blows her whistle and it quiets down a bit. "For style and flair above and beyond a typical spin or promenade—" She looks at her clipboard like we don't already know she's stalling to be funny. "Gordon and Zola!"

Gordon's unswollen eye starts to water. He clenches his fist into his body. "Yes!"

"Congratulations, Gordon and Zola," Coach says.

I fidget with my hands and bend my knees. My shorts ride up higher. In all the rush to clean my shoes, I forgot my spandex. My hair is spitting out in different directions. And there's a tiny water puddle by each of my feet. Today's vibe feels totally off from Friday, when I danced so well. If Papa's fêng shui thing applies to P.E. too, it's not looking promising.

"Last but not least. My favorite category." Coach snickers. "Most improved couple."

Couple?

My stomach pits out like I took a line drive straight to the gut. It's over. The final winner isn't some loser who convinced her brother to help her, or practiced alone in front of her mirror like a fool, thinking she could somehow win. I stare at my slushy feet. My shoes are getting blurry. I force myself not to blink.

Everyone is chattering. No one else even cares about what Coach is about to say.

Gordon's hand brushes my arm. "Sorry, Lupe."

I don't look up. The babbling is getting louder.

Coach blows her whistle. "Quiet! Next one to talk is running laps."

Now, not only is it dead silent, no one is even breathing. I hold perfectly still.

"Like I said, for most improved . . ." From the crumpling noise, she's obviously shuffling papers around needlessly. ". . . and I might add this also applies to attitude," she says. "The final winner . . . Lupe Wong!"

I blink. A tear rolls down each cheek. Mouth ajar, I turn my head toward Gordon and Niles.

Gordon makes a fist pump and starts laughing.

198

Jordyn and the soccer girls are laughing too, but not in the same way Gordon is. Niles leans out of line and beams a huge grin at me.

I glance over at Andy. I think I even see her smile a little, but she doesn't look at me.

"Are you kidding?" Samantha Pinkerton steps out of line and points at me. "Lupe doesn't even have a partner."

Coach walks toward the bleachers and sets down her clipboard, sniffing deeply. "Well thanks to Lupe, hopefully that will never happen again. From now on, people can switch up any time we need to even things out. And people will be able to choose whomever they want to dance with."

Samantha jostles her head from side to side. "Well, maybe I choose to dance with someone more professional."

"Shut up, Samantha!" Blake says, like someone who's just realized he's about to dance alone.

Coach snaps her head toward Samantha. "I believe I said next one to talk..."

Samantha's mouth drops open.

"Get to running," Coach says. "The rest of you, partner up."

Samantha stomps off for show, then paces into the slowest jog humanly possible. Everyone moves onto the gym floor with their partners and splits off into groups.

Blake walks toward Coach. "Can I practice with Lupe if Samantha can't be my partner?"

Coach Solden looks over at me. I'm still in shock from the announcement and haven't moved.

For a second it looks like she's going to make me dance with Blake. Then ... "I think you're both good on your own today," she says, giving me a quick wink.

She's right. I am good on my own.

Blake sulks away to try a full class of air-dancing. At least he won't have anyone to stomp on now that he's on his own.

But I can't do it. Even if he didn't have my back, I have his. "Blake," I call after him. I run up to him, and put my arm through his elbow. His slouch straightens, and he has a huge grin on his face.

Coach shakes her head but doesn't say anything. The phone on the wall rings. Coach hits play on the stereo. "Get to work everyone!"

People are already in groups and start dancing around.

Coach jogs over to the phone and picks it up. "Yes?" She shifts her body away, and I can't hear what she's saying.

When she turns back around she's staring at me with her brow furrowed. "What?" That part I can hear. She pauses. "I had no idea." She closes her eyes and shakes her head. "Of course. Let me work on this. Thank you for letting me know." Coach scans across the gym like she's mulling something over, then stops. Her eyes shift toward Carl, who's reaching above his head, chiseling who-knows-what from under the bleachers. She smiles, hanging up the phone. "Trondson, front and center!" Carl walks slowly toward her, gum bucket and chisel in hand.

Carl's eyes get wider the closer he gets to Coach, and his limp is suddenly more exaggerated.

She puts a hand on his shoulder like she did to me when she was giving me a pep talk.

Shoulders slumped, Carl hands her the chisel and bucket.

Coach catches me staring. "Blake, Lupe!" she yells. "Get going."

I jump. In all the excitement, I'd almost forgotten. I grin like I just busted open my birthday piñata. I think for a second Coach is mad, but when I glance at her, she has a satisfied grin on her face.

That's it. I did it. I got my A in P.E. I already have As in all the rest of my classes. I'm going to meet Fu Li. The only thing left—

My legs turn to Jell-O. How did I forget? Now, I have to square dance alone in front of the entire school.

CHAPTER 22

After a class of epic dancing with me leading Blake, I'm filled with a mix of terror and complete happiness. I also can't stop wondering what change Principal Singh has planned. Zola and I are the last ones walking toward the locker room because Gordon insisted on trying an added dip-spin at the end of the dance. He said I needed to try the move as well to see how it would play out on stage.

Zola pats my shoulder. "This is going to be awesome, Lupe."

My instinct is to glance at the spot on my shoulder she just touched. I don't, so I must be getting better at thinking she isn't just that kid who picks her nose every second of the day.

We round the corner into the locker room. I see Jordyn tossing an empty can of Hawaiian Breeze shaving cream to Andy.

Andy catches it, looking confused, but quickly throws it in the trash.

Jordyn makes an exaggerated wave. "Oh hi, Lupe."

Giggles echo through the locker room. I half expected a little teasing, but something feels off.

The closer I get to my locker, the stronger the scent of coconut gets. I look toward it, knowing it won't be good. The word *Guadapoopy* trails vertically down the center, the letters blending together. Fluffy white globs drip on the tile floor in front of my locker.

My face turns hot. Zola isn't laughing.

Zola whispers, her voice quivering, "They're just jealous."

I turn to look at her. Her eyes are welling up. "Sorry," she says. "I know how it feels."

My face gets even hotter. If Zola felt the same punch to the gut in the second grade that I'm feeling right now, it was my fault. She's looking at me like she and I are members of some club only we understand. And she's right. The rotten taste in my mouth must be from knowing I'm the one who put her in that club in the first place. Principal Singh's words suddenly make sense. *I did then what I knew how to do. Now that I know better, I do better.*

I stare around the room, not knowing what "better" should be. I meet Andy's eyes and she looks away. I've never felt so alone. I wish a sinkhole would suddenly open beneath me and swallow me whole.

Not everyone finds my locker as funny as Samantha, Claire, Jordyn, and their squads, but they're all still staring. The word *Guadapoopy* is now just a long streak going down my locker.

Coach walks in from the gym. The laughing suddenly stops. She stands behind Zola and me. She points at my locker. "Who did this?"

I open my locker to grab my towel, and dripping foam flings all over the floor. I start mopping up the tropical puddle.

Coach takes the towel from me. "Go ahead and change, Wong. I'll take care of this."

I try to keep my voice from shaking. "No, Coach. I can clean it up." I reach for the towel. "No big deal."

She ignores me and wipes down the center. The top layer of paint fades in one long streak.

"It *is* a big deal," she says loudly, staring back at the rest of the class. "I *will* find out who did this."

Coach spins back around and one foot slips on remnant shaving cream. Her foot flies up in the air, and she tries to catch herself with one arm. She falls to the floor with a thump and a small crack. Lips pursed together, noises burble from her mouth that sound like cusswords in an alien language.

Her garbles are mixed with giggling from around the locker room.

Why are some of them still laughing? She's hurt.

Zola and I aren't laughing. Neither is Andy. Andy is hurrying to get dressed, but I'm not sure if it's because she's trying to avoid me after helping trash my locker, or if she gets that this just went from a little prank to something more serious.

Coach cradles her left arm against her body. "When I find out who did this they'll pay with a week of detention!" She grunts, pushing herself to a seated position. "Everyone out!"

Now, everyone is shuffling to get dressed. Half the girls are already out the door. But I'm frozen. I stare down at Coach. It's one thing when you see a kid fall at school; when a grown-up who's supposed to be taking care of us gets hurt, it's a different kind of scary.

She's leaning against the bench, eyes closed, holding her arm. Andy grabs her things and runs after everyone else without even looking at me.

Coach cracks open an eye and sees me. "Go to class, Wong."

"Okay. I will," I lie.

I know I don't have permission, but I go to Coach's office and push the "Principal Singh" button on her phone.

"Yes, Becky?" Principal Singh answers.

"Not Becky. It's Lupe," I whisper. "We need help. Coach is hurt. I think she's delusional from the pain. Don't tell her I called you. But hurry up."

"On my way," she says, hanging up.

I stall, taking my time to get dressed. Principal Singh is there in less than two minutes, but the rest of the girls have already gone to their next class.

When Principal Singh runs toward her, Coach is still trying to wipe up shaving cream.

"Stop that, Becky," Principal Singh says.

"Oh, I'm fine," Coach argues. But her face looks as pale as a chalk line on the field.

I pick up my backpack to leave and scurry out of the locker room.

Jordyn is waiting, blocking my way. The scent of coconut surrounds her.

"What now?" I ask. "Haven't you done enough?"

She puts her hands on her hips and narrows her eyes. "If you say it was me, I'll say Andy was behind it."

My heart plummets to my ankles. "Why would you do that?"

She shrugs and walks toward the main building. "You heard Coach Solden. Someone has to pay the price."

***

Even though I know Andy was probably a little involved, and she isn't talking to me, the idea of her getting the entire blame for this makes me resent Jordyn, and Samantha, and all the follower bunheads, and the soccer club kids even more.

The day has had so many ups and downs, if I were Gordon, I'd for sure toss my breakfast back up.

I don't stop to chat with Delia, even when I see a new cat sitting in the middle of her catnip pot.

I take a shower and put on my PJs.

I don't know what makes me do it, but I check my email. It's been over a week, but the Change.org responses are up to three thousand total now. One hundred and forty-seven new emails are since last night alone. Subject lines scroll by like, "You have the backing of the ACLU-Florida chapter" and "Aren't you adorable!" and "I hated square dancing too!" But then, not only do I see more subject lines like, "Eradicate Square Dancing! Then kale!" but pledges. What?! It's not even supposed to be a fundraising site! Now on top of everything else, what the heck am I supposed to do with a bunch of money I don't deserve?

I hit close before I can see any more. I can't wrap my head around this right now on top of everything else.

I lie on my bed. I have no idea how to make this problem go away.

When I open my eyes, Mom is standing in my doorway.

"Sorry about today," she says. "Popcorn and *Doctor Who*?"

"Let me guess. Coach called."

"No, Principal Singh," she says.

"How's Coach?" I cross my arms over my eyes, trying to block out the visual of her lying on the locker room floor.

"She broke her arm. Six weeks in a cast, but she'll heal. Apparently there was an anonymous tip implicating someone."

This is worse than I thought. Coach breaking a bone just sent this to a code red. And Jordyn has already blamed Andy for what *she* did.

I turn onto my side toward Mom. "I'm not feeling so great. I'm going to go to bed early."

"You haven't even had dinner." She looks at me like I've lost my mind and puts her hand on my forehead. "You don't have a fever."

"Please." I can't fathom the idea of sitting at dinner when the entire universe is crashing down around me. "I'm not hungry."

Mom rubs my head. "Principal Singh emailed the link to the report you showed her. Why didn't you tell me?"

I still feel like I have moldy sardines in my mouth from the words in the song. "And have you see it too? You love all that dancing stuff. I don't want to ruin square dancing for everyone."

"Principal Singh sending the email was the right decision," she says. "It should be left for all the parents to decide whether or not to discuss it with their children."

Ice water runs up the back of my neck. "She sent it to *all* the parents?" I think of how hearing it made me feel, and imagine parents showing it to my classmates that very minute.

"Lupe, what you uncovered was a scab that needed to be peeled off. The most difficult issues to tackle are often the most uncomfortable to talk about. Do you think Principal Singh should approach this quietly? Or should we unveil what we've discovered so that everyone can learn and be more aware?"

I pull a pillow over my eyes. "Do you think Andy saw it?"

She peels the pillow away. "Andy's mom isn't the type to keep things from her, thinking she's protecting her. You guys should be given credit to see the good and the bad and try to find answers too."

But I don't have any answers to this one.

Mom tucks my hair behind my ear. "The past is confusing. A

lot of those people who did things like that just didn't know better. Kids called me names and teased me for being Mexican when I was young."

I think of the Krueger brothers calling me names and wonder why I've never told Mom about it.

"All we can do is give people a chance to learn and become better." Mom sighs. "Some will choose to do better. Some will never listen. But we can't ignore how some of those songs began, or no one will learn."

I think of Gordon, and how much he loves square dancing. And someone like Gordon would never say or do anything that might hurt anyone. "I guess square dancing isn't all bad," I say.

"It's not." Mom makes a cringeworthy kick out with her legs. "A partially crummy past isn't going to stop people from square dancing. We take the good parts, make them our own, and never repeat the bad parts."

I know she's probably right. And I feel a little better. But *Guadapoopy* is still etched in shaving cream in my mind too. I roll over. "Well, right now, I just want to sleep."

Mom leans down and kisses the side of my head. "Okay." She stops at my door on the way out. "You know, tomorrow will be better."

But something tells me it won't be.

If what my mom says is true, Andy is already in trouble.

Now, she'll get kicked off the soccer team. And on top of that, she'll probably get a week's detention and have to rebuild New Yack after her mom obliterates it. Andy will be in the doghouse

209

with her mom until she's old like our parents. I can't let this happen to her.

But I have no idea how to keep it from happening.

I imagine what would happen if I was the one Jordyn was targeting. Detention for me would be even worse.

If I had a week of detention, I'd miss practice. Our new coach was clear: miss three practices, and we lose our starting positions. I'd have to stare at Marcus's smug face from the bench most of the season if I was #2 in the rotation. There can't be much worse than that.

But what about Andy? All she wants is to make her mom proud of her.

I'm not sure what I can do to help. Papa said I don't always have to fight. Sometimes I have to overcome. How can I fight against Jordyn, but still find a way to overcome this so Andy doesn't get in trouble?

Suddenly everything I've been so focused on is nowhere close to as important as helping Andy. I'd give up anything to get her out of this. I lie on my side, staring at the sleeved Fu Li card on the wall. What would my dad do?

I'm not even pitching, but he comes in loud and clear.

Pitching to contact might not get you a perfect game, but making sacrifices to do what's best for your team is the most important thing.

I take deep breaths. I'm not sure if it's Dad's words, or Papa's fêng shui.

But I know what I have to do.

CHAPTER 23

I barely have time to brush my teeth. If I wait for Niles to walk to
school, there'll be too many kids and too much commotion by
the time we get there. I need Principal Singh to have her focus
on me.

I call Niles and tell him I'm going early to school so his mom
or dad can drive him instead. I leave Mom a note telling her I
had to leave early for a study group. It's a mini lie, but too much
is at stake to worry about a few fibs today. I run most of the way.

I wipe the sweat from my forehead before I knock on her
door. Déjà vu.

"Yes?" Principal Singh says.

I've brought every last manner I have with me for this one. I
open the door a tiny bit and poke my head in. "It's Lupe again.
May I please talk to you?"

She's rolling up her mat, so she looks extra calm. "Of course." She motions for me to come in. "Is this about what happened in P.E. yesterday?"

I put one hand in my pocket and cross my fingers, even though I know it doesn't make what I'm about to say less of a lie. I decide to blurt it out before she tells me her side of the story first. "I'm the one who put the shaving cream on my locker."

Principal Singh takes an extremely long drink from her water bottle and folds her hands on her desk. "You did, did you?"

"Yes." I keep my voice steady. "Whoever told you Andy did it lied. Andy didn't do it."

She leans way back in her big leather chair and narrows her eyes at me. "Interesting. I don't think I ever brought up Andalusia's name to anyone."

Pinpricks run up my scalp. I have one shot at this, and I'm blowing it. "Well, it was me. I did it."

"To your own locker?" she asks.

"I know it seems pointless," I say. "But I've looked it up. My frontal cortex isn't fully formed. I'm expected to make poor choices."

She sighs and shakes her head. "Lupe, you do know I have to give detention to the person responsible?"

"Yes, I understand."

What kid admits to trashing their own locker? Especially when everyone knows it wasn't them. I probably just guaranteed my outcast status for the next two years as well.

"Are you sure it was you?" she asks.

212

I can't look her in the eye. "I thought if I trashed my own locker . . ."

"Yes?" She motions for me to finish my statement.

"That . . ."

"Yes?"

"That, people would feel bad for me, and realize baseball was better than soccer."

Principal Singh's brow furrows. "What does that even mean?"

I think I was doing great up until the last part. I need to just keep to the facts—I acted alone.

"I know. It's a dumb reason. But I did it, by myself, so I have to pay the price." I bow my head and pretend to be ashamed.

"Well, I can't say I'm not baffled. But I don't have a choice," she says. "You'll have detention after school this week for destruction of school property."

I smile, but quickly bite my lips together, like the grin was a nervous reaction. "I understand."

Principal Singh writes up a detention slip and pushes it in front of me.

"You know if you sign that, you are saying it was you. I have to believe you if you say so."

"Yes." I take the paper and pen a little too eagerly and sign the bottom before she changes her mind. Even as I'm signing the paper, a burning pain twists in my gut knowing what else this means besides helping Andy. *What's best for my team is the most important thing . . .*

And just like that, I've sacrificed my #1 spot for the year.

***

Even though I only tell Niles about my fake confession, and he doesn't breathe a word, by Wednesday morning, word somehow gets around that I confessed. Word also gets around that it was a complete lie. At least ten people saw Jordyn do it. The result is not what I expected. Almost everyone, including my baseball team (even Marcus, but not because he feels sorry for me), is being a little nicer to me.

Principal Singh says "what I did" has nothing to do with the assembly, so I'm still dancing solo on stage Friday morning. She still hasn't revealed what her plan is to make square dancing any better.

On the way to P.E., Zola walks with me, Gordon, and Niles like we're all old buddies. Zola holds up a Snapchat of a kid do-si-do spinning his dog. And we see two seventh graders prome-nading before a math test for good luck. We've all been infected. Eventually, we'll be clomping around and terrorizing our children just like our parents.

I know now. I never stood a chance against square dancing.

Andy is already dressed and standing by our gym lockers when I get to P.E. Her face is droopy, but for now at least she's looking me in the eye. She's picking at her hangnail.

"Why would you confess to something we both know you didn't do?"

I drop my backpack and open my striped locker, which smells mildly of coconut. I bet Andy doesn't even know

Jordyn tried to throw her under the bus. "I don't know. I guess . . ."

Coach blows one long, louder-than-usual blast on her whistle. Thank goodness for her timing. I have no idea what I was going to say to Andy.

Coach is standing in her office doorway holding the whistle with her one good hand, a UW purple-and-gold-striped cast on the other. "Listen up. As you all know, we will end the square dancing section with our grand finale Salmon Days assembly Friday morning."

Everyone cheers, but I'm not sure if it's for the cool stuff we get to do on Salmon Days, or because we won't be square dancing anymore in P.E. "So take your stinky clothes home, as we won't be having P.E. tomorrow." She drops the whistle and points to me. "Wong! In my office!"

I hurry to yank on the loaners because I forgot mine. Again. Some things actually don't ever change.

Andy grins at me. It's just a small smile, but I haven't seen her look at me that way in a while. "Hold on." Andy reaches in her locker and hands me her soccer shorts.

I look away and blink back tears. "Thanks," I say, taking the shorts from her hand.

"My mom got the email from Principal Singh," she says, closing her locker. "You were the student who found the song?"

I nod.

"Why didn't you tell me?" she asks.

"We haven't exactly been talking." I pretend to tie my shoe, so

I don't have to look Andy in the eye. "And . . . the words were really bad."

"I heard," she says.

I look up and she holds my eyes. In the few seconds our eyes meet, a lot more passes between us than any words we might try to say.

"I'm just glad you told someone." She bends down to lock her locker. "Thanks, Lupe." She glances up and smiles.

I can tell we aren't even close to our old selves. But we'll get there.

"Wong!" rings in my ears from the direction of Coach's office.

"Coming, Coach!"

I'm pretty sure Coach knows I didn't coconut-cream my own locker. But if she does think I did it, then she also thinks I'm responsible for her broken arm.

I'm nervous about what to expect, but Coach doesn't look mad at all. I don't say anything. I stand in front of her, not knowing what to do with my hands, so I tuck them under my armpits.

"I can't for the life of me figure out why you'd admit to something I know you didn't do." She takes a pencil and scratches the inside of her cast. "Tell me this, did you have a good reason?"

I dig my hands into my sweaty armpits. "If I say anything, it doesn't mean I'm saying I didn't do it. Right?"

"Sure," she says. "Whatever."

I imagine Andy's mom's disappointment if she thought Andy was involved even a little. "Yep. I had a good reason."

216

CHAPTER 24

Of course, Coach Solden still rats me out to my mom and tells her she knows I didn't do it. Mom gives me trash, dishwasher, and Azteca cleaning duty that week for lying to Principal Singh. She says something about consequences.

Principal Singh announces Thursday morning that instead of replacing the annual Field Day with the Sadie Hawkins gender-neutral square dancing event (which of course was my fault), we'll be having our school's first annual Family Celebration of Cultures Night Friday evening to include everyone (in a way, also my fault). But I think Principal Singh's efforts to make things more inclusive of everyone is a step in the right direction. I think of how when this entire thing started, Andy pointed out that no one culture was any more important than another. What would have happened if I'd listened and we'd just gone to Principal Singh with this revelation in the beginning? Too late now.

I finish the third day of my detention, trying not to think about Marcus smirking up there on the mound. What's done is done.

Friday morning, I wake up way too early without an alarm. I know it's because I'm anxious for the assembly. I go outside in my PJs. I throw ten curves, ten changeups, and three knuckleballs for focus.

I know better, but I check my email again. It's up to 2,874 total. I can't even look when "I just broke my piggy bank to support your cause!" pops up in the subject line. I close it quickly.

I scamper into my room to find Mom standing there.

She has a ridiculous smile on her face. She pulls cowboy boots from behind her back.

"Nope," I say.

"Listen. You have to play the part. The school portal said to wear dancing duds." She raises the boots up in the air like they are some magical relic.

I point to my broken-in, Gordon-vomit and mud-christened shoes. "I have a system. I'll fall off the stage in those things."

"Fine, but . . ." She pulls my overalls off the bed from behind her, goofy smile back. They're plastered with red-checkered patches.

"Mawwwwwm! What did you do?" I'd planned on wearing my overalls for the assembly, but now I have no time to plan a new outfit or cut off the patches.

218

"We can take them off when it's over." She holds them in front of me to put my legs in like when I was a kid. "I didn't get to do this with Paolo," she says.

"Yeah, because they didn't have a stupid assembly!"

She ignores me and pulls them up to my waist.

Paolo walks in carrying a sombrero.

This isn't happening.

Mom waves her hand at him like he's some incompetent assistant. "No, no! The straw hat."

Paolo stomps back toward the garage.

"How about *no hat*?!" I say.

Her voice is way higher than usual, and she claps her hands quickly. "You are going to look so authentic."

Just wait till she sees me dancing alone while the rest of the kids are partnered up. She's way too happy for something that's going to disappoint her.

"You do remember I'm going to stick out like a beacon up there by myself." I stand up and my overalls fall to my knees.

"Oh, I know." My mom smiles and helps me pull my pants back up. She buttons the strap on my overalls. "And you will be the most magnificent beacon on that stage." She kisses my cheek.

Paolo walks back in. The hat he's carrying is definitely straw. The edges have twigs darting out like hillbilly tassels.

"Really, I don't want a hat." It's a fine line between letting moms feel useful and not hurting their feelings. "I mean any other hoedown I would, but I need to be able to see really well."

"Pffft," she mutters, and grabs a brush off my nightstand.

219

You'd think my mom would be more miffed by me dancing alone than me refusing to wear the dumb hat.

She parts my hair and makes a French braid down each side of my head instead. She reaches in her pocket and holds up a tube of mascara.

"Nope!"

She tilts her head, eyes wide, like she can't believe I'm upset. "It's for freckles."

I fold my arms over my chest.

"Fine." She slips it back in her pocket and adjusts the collar on my shirt.

I run my hands over the patches on my overalls and let out a deep sigh.

"You know, Becky Solden didn't have a great experience with square dancing when we were your age."

"Well, it couldn't have been as bad as dancing in front of the whole school," I say.

"Oh, it was worse."

"Really?" I ask.

"Yeah. Really." Mom isn't smiling.

She leans over and rolls my pant legs up to my shins. I'll just have to unroll them later when she's not watching.

"Well, are you going to tell me?" I ask.

She sits next to me. "One by one, as a joke, the boys approached her, then passed her by for other girls. She was the last girl, but a kid named Bruce was still left."

With a name like Bruce I already know this can't end well.

"Just like the rest, he walked up to her, but he stopped and bowed. She was already mortified, but she still reached out to take his hand like the teacher told us we had to."

"What's the big deal? Lots of people had horrible partners."

"It didn't end there. Just before Becky touched his hand, Bruce jumped back and ran toward the boys' locker room screaming. Everyone laughed . . . except Becky."

"So? Didn't he just get in trouble and still have to dance with Coach?" I ask.

"Well, the teacher told him exactly that—to go run two laps and hustle to get back to dance with Becky. To which Bruce said he'd rather do detention than dance with an ape."

Even decades later, my heart aches a little for Coach. "So then what?"

"Bruce got detention, and Becky was on her own." Mom's voice sounds like if they were right there in front of us, she'd hug Coach and kick Bruce in the unmentionables.

I was left out by default. Coach Solden was humiliated. "That *is* horrible." I pick at a checkered patch on my knee. "But it's still not as bad as having to dance alone in front—"

"It gets worse. For the entire two weeks we danced, every time a boy danced with Becky, he made monkey noises under his breath. You know, 'ooh-ooh, eeeeh-eeeeh.' Even some of the girls made monkey noises and pretended to scratch their armpits."

Maybe Coach insisting I dance on my own was the result of some sort of wound she was holding onto for thirty years. Now I

221

know why she had the far-off look when she was talking about "someone always has to dance alone" and all that "it will build your character" stuff.

Even with what Samantha, Jordyn, and the others did to me, it wasn't *that* humiliating. "Wow," I say.

"Yeah. Middle school sucked for us too, Lupe."

The doorbell rings.

"It's Niles." My heart pounds. We'd already arranged this. Today more than any other day is one where we need safety in numbers.

"I'll get it." Mom stands and kisses my forehead. "You are going to be amazing, Lupe." She walks toward the door.

I sit on the floor, tie my shoes, and unfold the rolled hems. When I look up, Andy's standing in my doorway holding a puffed-out Hefty bag. Her forehead is all sweaty and she's biting her lower lip.

"Hey," I finally say.

She doesn't answer.

"So . . . what's up?" I ask.

"I didn't know where else to go," she says. She reaches in the Hefty bag and pulls out a dress with ruffles wider than the doorframe. A blast of *Encouragement* hits me in the face.

"Oh no," I whisper. "Niles's mom made this."

"How'd you know?"

The dress is covered in blue and gold. Men's torsos are tilted in different directions all over the skirt. One guy with straight black bangs plastered to his head is wearing a skintight, Smurf-blue, long-sleeved shirt. I recognize him as one of the people on Niles's new *Star Trek* poster in his room. He's waving . . . I think. It's the same hand-cramp gesture Niles signaled to Gordon making his pinky and ring finger look glued together.

"She was just so excited about the idea. She asked Niles if it was okay . . . Then he asked me . . ." Andy sighs. "She was so happy about the outfits, we felt too guilty saying no."

This is bad. They are both really going to need me once the kids at school get a look at their outfits.

I tilt my head sideways, trying to figure out the hand signal. "Is he making dog shadows?"

The other guy in puke-gold is narrowing his eyes like he's flirting and holding what looks like an antique flip phone.

Andy's voice sounds tiny. "It's Spock and Captain Kirk."

"*Star Trek*?" I ask.

"Yes. TOS," she answers.

"TOS?"

"The Original Series."

"It'll be okay. No one will even notice the weird dudes with how far away we'll be from the audience."

"Maybe." Andy holds up the skirt, and it bumps into my head. "But I'll take up half the stage in this thing."

She has a point. She plops down next to me. After her third awkward sigh, she says, "Lupe, why'd you say it was you?"

I shrug. "I don't know. Can we just talk about it later?"

"I know Jordyn was going to let me take the blame," she says.

I jerk my head toward her. I only mentioned Jordyn's threat to one person. "How'd you know that?"

"Niles told me."

"Oh."

"Why though?" she asks again.

I can't help the quick glance at my glove at the end of my bed. I try not to imagine sitting the bench and watching Marcus pitch. "I guess I thought you had more to lose than me," I say, dropping my head to my chest. "And I'm really sorry about what I said about your mom, and coding classes, and soccer, and peeing your pants—"

"Well, I quit the soccer team," Andy interrupts.

"What?" I should be happy. But now I can only think that maybe what I did for Andy was for nothing.

Andy stares at the floor, picking her thumbnail. "I told Jordyn not to speak to me again, so of course, no one else will talk to me either."

She doesn't have to say any more. Andy just self-destructed her social status.

"What about your mom? Didn't she say you had to play?"

"My mom had her chance to be a middle-schooler. Even though the way you said it was pretty mean, you were a little bit right. If my mom is only proud about the things she wants me to do, that's on her. But, I think dancing in front of the school today will make up for it a little."

I hope she's right and New Yack is intact.

We sit in silence for a bit.

"Being alone is no fun," I finally say.

Andy sniffs but I can't see her face.

"Sorry I didn't appreciate you," I say. "I won't do it again."

Andy takes my pillow and wipes her nose. I make a mental note to flip it inside out before I go to sleep.

She turns toward me, and boops me on the nose. I boop her back.

I reach into my bedside table, pull out a Ziploc bag, and hand it to Andy. Inside, there are two miniature landscape boulders, a shell I thought she could use as a dinner plate, and a mouse-sized white cowhide coat I cut out of a baseball cover I found at the field.

Andy grins, but now she's picking at her nail so hard I think she might hit bone any second. Her mouth opens and closes a few times like she can't spit out what she wants to say.

"What is it?"

Andy takes a deep breath. "I was wondering . . ." She stops.

I think of how her dad works so much. How her mom won't listen to her. "What were you going to say?" I ask.

The corners of her mouth turn up in a small smile. "There's a raptor convention at Seattle Center next weekend. Wanna go?"

I smile, teeth clenched. I'd rather lick a frog. "Sure. If that's what you feel like."

She sets her hands calmly in her lap. "It is."

If I'm going to be a better friend to Andy and Niles, I'll need to get used to owl puke and Comic-Con for them. She nudges me, and I stand holding my hand out for her. She takes it smiling, and I pull her up.

We lay her dress out on the floor, ruffles down. Andy holds my hand for balance, stepping one foot at a time into the waist hole like a game of Twister. I change her shoes for her because once the dress is on, she can't see her feet. We shove her through my door and into the living room.

Mom walks in and she flinches back when she sees Andy's dress. "Oh my!"

I lean back so Andy can't see me. I shake my head frantically at my mom.

Luckily my mom catches the hint. "What a lovely dress," she says.

Andy gives her a weak smile.

"You know, I'm going in your direction," Mom says.

I know it's a lie. Even my mom can see the torture we'd endure if we have to ride the bus.

I walk out the front door and find Niles standing at the gate waiting. He's wearing a button-up shirt with the same fabric as Andy's. He shrugs and makes a half smile when we see each other. Then Andy walks out after me. Niles fidgets a bit then walks quickly to stand next to her. He has the *Star Trek* pin on his shirt that matches her skirt. Next to each other, they look like lemon and blueberry Jolly Ranchers melded into a swirly human glob.

"What do you think?" Niles asks nervously.

Andy puts out her fist with a fierce squint in her eyes. "We got this."

Niles smiles and fist bumps her.

My mom unlocks the car doors. "Pile in, troops."

We stuff Andy in, and Niles and I sit on either side. Andy's skirt keeps scratching against my arm, so I tuck my jacket in between us.

When we get to school, we park in front, and Niles opens the door.

"Wait," I reach over and pull the door handle back. Kids are already walking in and the halls are filling up. I'm not ready.

Mom turns around in her seat. "You'll be fine. You all look wonderful." She activates her superpower and starts jiggling around and singing "Old Dan Tucker." For some reason, it's not as embarrassing as it would have been a few weeks ago.

Andy reaches over Niles and pushes the door further open. "Let's get this over with."

Niles nods at me. "She's right. You can stall all you want. Today is still gonna happen."

Andy shrugs behind him. "He's right."

We pull Andy out of the car. Her skirt expands like a gigantic Chinese fan.

Drop-off kids pass by. Most stare and smile. I know it's because they're glad they aren't us. Mr. Lundgren walks by wearing a fluorescent yellow shirt that says, "Think Like a

227

Proton. Stay Positive!" He gives us the thumbs-up. Not exactly the endorsement I was looking for.

A boy walks by and says, "Niiiiice." The three of us just look at each other and smile.

We stand in a row facing the school. The front windows stare back. And the double doors open wide like a mouth that wants to gobble us up for daring to come to school dressed like this.

CHAPTER 25

The curtain is closed. We're huddled together backstage. Of course, the four "couples" in our class are assigned to the front. I wonder if there's a fêng shui arrangement for square dancing.

Blake and Samantha stand next to each other. They're wearing what looks like a custom-order *Dancing with the Stars* ensemble. Samantha must have dance-outfit connections. And she obviously used them here. They both have the school colors of blue and green, cut like opposing diagonals across their bodies. Standing together, their outfits form a green triangle in the center. But they're no team. She yanks her shoulder away from him, and their triangle sags into a rhombus.

Coach is on the side of the stage giving instructions to Carl and another kid who is running the music. Apparently the mysterious phone call in P.E. was Principal Singh telling Coach about the bad lyrics I'd shown her and asking Coach if she had any ideas on how to help. Coach knew just the wart-footed victim who could add their own touch to "Turkey in the Straw." She even gave Carl "creative freedom" to write what he wants, as long as there are no cusswords or derogatory lyrics.

Zola's arms are wrapped around her waist. She's wearing blue gingham and looks like a recycled Dorothy from a *Wizard of Oz* Halloween costume. She's tapping her foot. "Where is he?" she mumbles.

Andy faces Niles, whispering to him. "We've done this a million times. We just pretend we're back in class, right?"

He gives her little nods. "Am I starting the count, or you?"

Andy takes two deep breaths. "I think you'd better do it."

I stand alone, wringing my hands. I close my eyes and visualize I'm dancing with Paolo.

"Hey guys." Gordon runs up, out of breath. He is the only one not wearing something countrified by his mom, grandma, or a professional seamstress. He has on black pants and a Sammy Sockeye sweatshirt. His hair is jutting out from beneath the science goggles on top of his head. He motions to Niles and Andy. "Well done. I see you're representing Starfleet." The swelling in Gordon's eye is down, but a crescent of black sits over his cheek.

Niles grins. He presses his pin, and it chirps.

Gordon slips the goggles onto his face.

"How's the eye?" I ask.

"It will heal. There's always a price for a man's growth, I suppose."

Niles nods in agreement.

Gordon pulls a red glittery hair bow out of his pocket. He presents it in both hands to Zola. "May I?"

She stops tapping her foot. She blushes as he pins it to her braid. The bell for first period rings.

Coach Solden, wearing a purple shirt to match her cast, blows her whistle from the front of the stage. She tries to tuck in her shirt but can't with her one good arm, and gives up. "All right, everyone. You all know your positions. We have about . . ." She looks at her watch. ". . . eight-and-a-half minutes."

My face prickles like my foot does when it falls asleep.

Andy's eyes are closed. She's breathing slowly in and out, arms straight at her sides like some sort of standing yoga pose. Niles squats just a bit into a modified version of his sumo wrestler pose. His mouth is moving, so I know he's getting in the zone too. Gordon is whispering to himself. "You are thpethial. You are thtrong."

The rumble of voices and footsteps echoes from the other side of the curtain.

Niles lets out a deep breath and stands upright. "How you feeling, Lupe?"

I stare through the small opening in the center of the curtain at the filling auditorium. "Pretty freaking scared."

"Would you rather hang from a burning rope over the Grand

Canyon filled with rattlesnakes or dance on stage in five minutes?" He smiles at me.

I can't help grabbing my stomach and closing my eyes. "Rattlesnakes."

The next thing I know, I'm nearly bowled over in a bear hug. I open my eyes and see Sammy Sockeye staring back. "It's okay, Lupe. You are thtrong too."

Then Andy is wrapped around Gordon and me. Then Zola. When the huddle breaks, Niles gives me a quick side squeeze.

That thing my mom told me about . . . how in middle school, I only needed one good friend to survive?

I have four.

Coach's whistle blows way quieter than usual. "On your marks, everyone."

Niles slips his earplugs from his pocket and puts them in. Gordon pulls his sweatshirt off over his head and tosses it dramatically to the side of the stage. Underneath is a black dress shirt. There's a collective gasp. It's bedazzled with red and white rhinestones. I squint and realize the rhinestones are in the shape of the *Millennium Falcon*. He turns his head toward Niles and they both laugh. Gordon puts his hands on his hips and a cape spreads out like butterfly wings between his shoulder blades and his wrists. Zola's smile and eyes are even bigger than the first time she saw him with his new clothes and hair.

Coach stares at Gordon's shirt, brow furrowed. "What?"

"Style and flair, Coach." He pushes a button on a little black box clipped to his belt. He lifts his wings and pinpoints of lights fill the black fabric. He spins, and between the stage lights, the rhinestones on Gordon's shirt, and his shimmering wings, the entire stage fills with magical glow orbs.

Red and white lights reflect in Coach's eyes. Her face goes as red as the orbs.

Gordon hits the button shutting down the power. "Soooo, not yet?"

Principal Singh's voice rings over the microphone. "Welcome, students, parents, city leaders, to our kickoff celebration of Issaquah Salmon Days . . ."

We all freeze, including Gordon. There's not a thing Coach can do about him now, so she shoos us into position and takes her spot behind the front left curtain next to me.

The microphone squeals. "Following Pin the Tail on Sasquatch, we will be bobbing for apples. After a logging demonstration, we'll break for some local blueberry pie . . ."

There are some *yums* and clapping.

"And," her voice rises, "a stroll to the salmon hatchery." The *yums* and claps stop abruptly.

"I'd like to also remind everyone that we come from all over the world," she continues. "Or have been here for thousands of years. So, as I've already announced, in lieu of Field Day or Sadie Hawkins, we'd like to remind and invite you all to our Family Celebration of Cultures Night this evening."

Two sets of claps ring out. One is Gordon next to me. Through the gap in the curtain, I see the other is a little old lady with a grey ponytail, sitting in the front row. Even with all her teeth, I'd recognize that smile anywhere. Grandma Schnelly.

"Yes. Very exciting," Principal Singh says. "But let's first take things back a few years, to a time before twerking, and when rap music was a gentleman calling out dance directions."

Coach Solden laughs backstage, but the audience is silent.

"Anyway . . ." Principal Singh continues, ". . . without further delay, I present to you . . ."

The tune for "Turkey in the Straw" with fiddles screeches in sync with plucked banjos.

"The Sockeye Square Dancers!"

The curtain opens. It's a packed house. And it's not just students filling the seats. Lots of people are standing along the aisles with the teachers. They pull out cameras and phones, and little red lights turn on. I focus and stare straight ahead. I remember to smile and hope it doesn't look like the half-petrified grimace from my kindergarten picture. I count down with the music. We start dancing in three . . . two . . .

The music stops. It's completely silent.

Andy and I glance first at each other, then at the side of the stage. Coach is running over to the kid with the stereo. Visible to the crowd, Carl is standing just to the side of the kid holding a microphone. The kid has the disc out and is wiping it on his sleeve. He huffs a breath on it and wipes it again like he's got all the time in the world.

Carl's voice cracks, "We . . . uh . . . appreciate your patience, y'all."

I stare back out at the audience, manufactured grin back on.

Jordyn and the other soccer girls are in the fifth row. They're elbowing each other and pointing toward Andy. She sees them too. She lifts her chin and looks away from them.

Coach grabs the disc out of the kid's hand and slips it back in the CD player.

I scan the audience. My mom didn't lie. She *was* going this way. She's sitting in the third row right in front of me. Paolo, Papa, Grandma Wong, and Bela are with her. I can't believe she pulled Paolo out of school for this. Paolo smirks and takes a picture of me with his phone. I'm pretty sure he just added to the embarrassing slide show at my wedding someday. Bela is smiling nervously with her hands folded over the huge purse in her lap. Papa Wong is wearing a tie, and Grandma Wong's had her hair done, which she only does for special occasions. I catch her eye and she gives me a small smile and a nod.

Half my baseball team is sitting together on the opposite side of the auditorium. They wave at me and Blake.

I turn to Blake to see if he saw them. He smiles and gives me the signal to hit away. The fiddles start up again, followed by the banjos.

Gordon hits his black button and lifts his wings for the audience. The audience erupts in "Oooohs, aaaaahs," and a few snickers.

I have to lean in past Gordon's wings to see Niles on the other side of him. Niles is stepping back and forth from one foot to another, and staring out at the audience like it's filled with velociraptors. I'm worried he might have a meltdown, and my instinct is to break out of line and go to him.

Andy pats him on the shoulder. "Are you sure you're cool with this, Niles?"

He nods. "Yep."

He turns to her, and I realize she's started counting in Klingon. "Wa', cha', wej, loS."

Niles mouths the same words back to her and stops swaying.

Coach holds up her one good hand, fingers counting down, "Three . . . two . . . one."

I tap my foot with her countdown. Here we go.

Carl's voice rings out with the tune. "Honor your partner."

The boys and I all bow. The girls curtsy.

"Twirl your partner."

The stage vibrates with our steps. I put out my elbow for my imaginary partner and spin her into our group. We aren't as precise as Riverdance, but our steps boom through the theater like a bass drum.

The music is way louder than in the gym and it's harder to hear, but I know the routine and imagine I'm with Paolo in the living room. I'm actually having fun and almost forget where I am.

Carl takes a few limped steps toward the center stage, and when the familiar chorus arrives, words not remotely resembling the actual lyrics come out of his mouth . . .

"Warts were in my heel, now they're in a jar. Warts were in my heel, now they're in a jar, Scoop 'em out, preserve 'em, Shake 'em up like salt."

He holds up the glass vial and shakes it. The two chunks slam around in the formaldehyde.

"Warts were in my heel, but now they're in a jar."

I don't even know what I'm hearing. The audience looks confused too. Principal Singh did it. I will forever hear Carl's wart rap any time I hear this tune.

"Do-si-do, amigos," Carl calls out.

Gordon spins, and his rhinestones and lights create little twinkles across the stage. He's either causing one heck of a laser light show or a room full of migraines. With Zola in her checkered blue-and-white dress, and red-sequined hair bow next to him, they do look a little like Dorothy and a light-up Wizard.

Niles and Andy are in perfect form as a team, counting in sync with every footstep, spin, and twirl. I get what Niles meant about it being similar to his martial arts form, but they're a lot more graceful. I twirl my pretend Paolo while Niles spins Andy.

Samantha is sneering at Blake, who's accidentally snagged her hair between his fingers.

When we turn, I have a view of Coach Solden. As always, she's doing every dance move along with us by herself.

Always someone left to dance alone.

No more. Before the caller can yell out for us to twirl our partners again, I run over to Coach along the side of the stage. She motions for me to go back. Instead, I bow and hold out my hand. She won't take my hand. Is she hearing monkey noises somewhere deep down inside? The first rule she taught us is we *have* to accept the invitation. She's not accepting.

She must be in shock. I reach out, take her good hand from her side, and pull her out on stage with me before she can argue. I hear some claps from the audience.

She joins the group with Gordon, Zola, Niles, Andy, Samantha, Blake, and me.

Carl beatboxes, then sings out again. "Scoop it up, preserve it, shake it like salt . . ."

Coach smiles nervously as I twirl her.

"Switch up, cowpokes," Carl says.

We switch partners and now Coach is with Niles.

Gordon twirls Andy and clotheslines her neck with his wing. But they shake it off and continue. He dips her and she flings out an arm and leg in true flourish form.

Carl yells out. "Back with your partners."

We switch back and Andy picks up counting right along with Niles.

I ticktock my head like Coach, and we do-si-do around each other, kicking our feet out. She's bobbing her head in sync with mine.

"Little bit o'wart heal, little bit o' toe, promenade and don't be slow," Carl says.

We go into group-circle promenade like it's habit. It's too loud to hear, but some of us are laughing. Niles and Andy are still counting, "Wa', cha', wej . . ."

"Lady goes right, gent goes left. Right around, so breezy. Make the arch and make it high and pop them through so easy."

Niles and Andy go through the arch, but Andy's skirt gets stuck. Gordon and Zola are so focused they don't realize Andy's wedged tight between them. Coach and I break our arch and shove Andy from behind, Niles pulls her from the front, and her skirt breaks through.

Now the audience is laughing over all the music and dance stomping. But we are all laughing too, including Coach.

"All in to the center and back."

Coach and I meet at the middle of our circle with the rest of our group, and she clearly snorts.

"Allemande left."

We each turn to the person next to us and hold out our left arms, spin, and then go back to our original spots.

"Aces high, Deuces low. Promenade and away you all . . . go . . . home. . . ."

Carl purses his lips together for freestyle beatbox. The last banjo rings out. He waves one arm in the air with the finale. "Dong, dee, dee, donk, donk."

"Yee-haw!" Gordon yells, and chucks his goggles into the air.

We face the applauding audience. Out of the entire audience, Grandma Wong stands first. She clasps her hands above her head in a cheering motion. Paolo slumps further in his seat. Mom, Bela, and Papa Wong stand too, joining Grandma, and they clap loudly with the rest of the crowd.

I see Papa Wong has a bag of sunflower seeds jutting out of his pocket. We won't need those today.

Gordon bows to Zola, and I almost forget to thank my partner.

I take Coach's hand and bow to her.

She curtsies back. When she stands upright, there are tears in her eyes.

I might like square dancing.

CHAPTER 26

Seven hours later, I blend in like a potato in a bowl of fruit, wearing my cutoffs and T-shirt in a crowd of amazing outfits.

Principal Singh's purple sari with gold embroidery wraps around a bright orange undershirt. Her voice squeaks out nervously over the loud speaker. "Family and friends. We've had a much larger turnout than anticipated for our first annual Family Celebration of Cultures Night. So, we will need to move from the cafeteria to the field for cultural performances."

People scurry out the door toward the track like excited ants. I wish I were heading home to pitch into my net so I can get my #1 position back next year. But even though I'd rather be practicing knuckleballs, it feels sorta good to see everyone so happy.

Gordon stuffs his fourth lumpia from the Filipino platter into his mouth, and he's already eaten six of Grandma Wong's ha gao.

Andy and I exchange nervous glances.

"Hey Gordon," Andy says. "You planning on dancing some more tonight?" Andy must be having the same flashback.

"You bet!" he says.

I can't help the involuntary peek down at my shoes. A fleck of yellow breakfast sludge is still embedded in one of my shoelaces.

Zola hands us each an Irish shortbread cookie, and we all walk outside toward the field. Niles and his parents are sitting on a bench off to the side, where it's a little quieter, away from the crowd. His dad is reading a book with a cover so creepy it can only be that King guy.

There's no sign of any of my baseball team. No surprise, since it's no longer Field Day. And thankfully, Jordyn and most of the soccer girls aren't here either.

Samantha Pinkerton has cordoned off an area with soccer cones and is already on the field twirling and spinning in her stiff, sparkly tutu like this event was made for her.

Coach Solden holds a megaphone up to her mouth. "Thank you all for coming. Since we're on a streak, we're going to continue the night with, what else . . . more dancing."

Principal Singh snickers, and I'm pretty sure they're the only ones who find each other funny.

Coach continues, "So, we'll start things off with a lively dance originating in the Czech Republic." She nods to Gordon.

242

Gordon wipes his mouth and hands me the dirty napkin. "That's my cue." He approaches the lady I recognized as his grandma and takes off his hoodie. He tosses it aside in what I now think is going to be his signature pre-performance move. Underneath he's wearing a velvet vest with embroidered poppies that matches his grandma's skirt and vest. Curly ribbons trail down her grey ponytail.

Gordon walks to the center of the field holding her hand. A man with a super perfect smile, carrying an accordion, gazes adoringly at Gordon's grandma. The man (must be the boyfriend) spreads his arms back and forth, moving air through the accordion.

People gather around in a wide circle. Anyone who might have been mildly interested is no longer paying attention to Samantha Pinkerton. She stomps off the field past Andy, Zola, and me in a flowery breeze, her bun unraveling along the way.

A humming twang echoes over the field as the boyfriend flicks his fingers across little piano-looking keys. The crowd claps their hands as Gordon and his grandma spin and kick in perfect rhythm. Their arms fling out in a synchronized windmill flourish to the accordion. I imagine the grease and shrimp concoction centrifuging around in Gordon's guts. But his color still looks good.

Gordon twirls his grandma around in a final frenzy until the song ends. They bow.

Whoops and hollers ricochet over the field, only dying down

when Coach Solden's megaphone screeches. Half the people grab their ears.

"Pardon me." Coach clears her throat like that will make the megaphone operate properly. "Next, Andalusia Washington and her family will perform a dance from Guinea where Andalusia's grandfather was born."

What? I realize I've lost track of Andy. I scan the field and see Andy and her brother already moving toward the center of the field. They're carrying drums. Andy sits on a stool, a drum almost as big as her placed directly in front. Her little brother plops down next to her with a smaller drum.

A woman steps out, and after a second, I realize it's Andy's mom. But it can't be her. She's not wearing a suit, high heels, or Spanx leggings. A long brightly colored dress wraps around her waist. Andy starts to beat on the drum and her brother joins in.

"We will be performing a West African harvest dance called kassa," Mrs. Washington announces, and begins swaying her hips.

I cringe and look at Andy. Funny thing, she doesn't look embarrassed at all.

Andy's mom closes her eyes and moves her head to the drumbeat. She steps from side to side, her feet moving faster and faster. The drumbeat keeps up with her feet. She dips down moving her arms in sweeping motions from side to side. Between the vibration of Andy's drumming in my chest, and Mrs. Washington moving so freely, I have goose bumps. It's sort of . . . beautiful.

How come Andy never told me she played the drum? Have I not shared something about myself with Andy? She's met most of my relatives, but I realize there are things about both sides of my family I've thought she wouldn't understand. Like, I've never taken Andy to dim sum, because I thought she'd be weirded out by stuff I'm used to, like the chicken feet or tripe. I've avoided taking her to Bela's because I knew we'd get stuck watching telenovelas for hours. Or how I steered her away from the ofrenda for Dad on Diá de los Muertos because I was afraid she wouldn't understand and think it was morbid.

I just didn't give her the chance.

Andy's family finishes, and Mom and I wait until the cheering stops.

I hug Andy, then stand in front of her mom. "That was really amazing, Mrs. Washington."

Mrs. Washington's eyes look a little teary. "Thank you, Guadalupe." She wipes her brow and gives a relaxed smile. "Would you like to come dance with us sometime at the house?"

"I . . . I . . ." I'm not even sure how to backtrack out of this one.

"Then it's decided. We'd love to have you over next week to dance with us."

I look to Andy for help and she just laughs. I have a hard enough time ditching my mom and her dancing. Now I have to ditch Andy's mom too?

Coach announces, "Now, our own Principal Singh and her son, Rajesh, will be performing a hip-hop Indian dance."

Principal Singh steps out with a boy in a matching outfit. He's

245

a mini version of her, mimicking her exact moves just like the Bollywood dancers I've seen on TV.

An eighth grader and his little sister stomp and spin the jarabe tapatío after them. It's a dance I sort of know how to do, but there's no way in heck I'm participating.

"Oh, look. The Mexican hat dance," someone's dad calls out incorrectly. I think this night has already made a ton of progress, so I decide not to tell him. This time.

A van with *Chinese Senior Center* on its side panel pulls up next to the field a little later, and my grandpa gets out of the passenger seat. He waves to me across the field.

I whistle to Coach getting her attention. "They're here," I mouth.

Coach nods and lifts up the megaphone. "Ahem. Three ... two ..."

The students are already quiet by "two." The grown-ups follow suit and stop what they're doing, even though their grades aren't at risk.

"I'd like to thank Guadalupe Wong's grandfather for arranging a special treat," Coach says.

The sliding door to the van opens. Four men, two with drums, two with cymbals, emerge. The men move toward the field pounding on the drumheads bare-handed. The men with cymbals follow, clanking them together every so often, then picking up the speed.

The crowd stares with wide eyes at the four men. I grin, knowing the people are all looking in the wrong direction.

A large feathery head of what looks like a friendly red dragon emerges from the sliding door of the van. A few people notice and gasp. Next to the red head, a second yellow head pops out. They jump out of the van, their hind ends still inside. With large blinking eyes, the heads start bobbing back and forth to the beat of the drums and cymbals. The back sections of the bodies emerge from the van in a slithery ripple. Even though the heads look like dragons, they're actually lions. The red and yellow heads jump around the field to the drumbeat of the lion dance, flapping their eyes and mouths at people who scream and laugh at the same time.

The dance is magical, and colorful and mysterious. I smile, thinking those are some of the things I'm made of.

The cymbals are earsplitting and the thud of the drums thumps in my chest. I turn toward Niles and his parents back on the bench, but he's still got his earplugs in and grins back at me.

I turn again to see the dragons zigzag their way around the crowd, then back to the van. I run after them and hug Papa. "Thank you," I say into his chest.

He sits back in the van, motioning toward the field. "This is what happens when you overcome instead of fighting."

As I watch Papa drive away, Principal Singh stands next to me and nudges me with her elbow. "So, what do you think, Lupe?"

I know this was her resolution to make dancing more inclusive. Still, I stare out at the crowd and wish every school activity could include everyone. "It's a good start."

"Start?" she asks.

"Tonight has me thinking about the father-daughter winter dance?"

She scans the crowd. She must see what I do—lots of families with single moms and single dads, two families with two moms, three with two dads.

"Point taken. I guess we have more work to do." She sighs and pats me on the back. "Raj! No!" She blurts out. She disappears in a colorful blur chasing after her son, who's just picked a half-eaten gyoza off the turf and stuffed it into his mouth.

I hear a familiar sound, and sure enough, it's salsa music blaring. Mom's superpower is out in full force. She's got poor Mr. Lundgren by the waist. He's wearing an "All the Good Science Puns Argon" shirt. He's sweating just like in lab, but it's a cool night. Mom's trying to help him shift his hips smoothly, but they rock stiffly back and forth.

It's getting dark, but no one is leaving. The field is packed with all different types of dancing that mesh together perfectly. All a little different. Some of us aren't even *from* here. And some of us were right here before this country existed. But none of us are any better than the other.

Niles's dad sets his book down and waves as I approach. His mom smiles. Niles's earplugs are still in, so I hold my hand out offering him a dance.

Instead of accepting the offer, Niles points toward the people on the field.

I turn to see what he sees. Crowds of people eating and

248

dancing and having fun. I think of how stubborn I was, and how I never would have appreciated this all a month ago. But now . . .

When I turn back around, Niles stands and plants a Little Dragons Post-it note on my forehead. I laugh and peel it off. I hold it in my hand. Black block letters on bright pink stare back at me. "You are brave." Something catches in my throat. I look up at him, and Niles is standing and offering his hand to me. I smile and accept without even thinking about it. Being asked by a boy isn't so bad.

We find Mom and Mr. Lundgren and dance next to them.

CHAPTER 27

Even though it wasn't meant to be a fundraiser, my Change.org effort raised almost $12,000 in donations. Mostly because people thought it was "cute." Square dancing still exists. I'm actually happy I didn't succeed in ending it. But I'm even gladder Principal Singh helped figure out a way to learn from it and make changes for our school.

Plus, now, we can dance with whoever we want. It didn't feel right to keep the money, so I gave it to Fu Li's foundation, which sounded pretty cool.

What does all that mean? Turns out I never even had to make the straight As deal with Uncle Hector. Fu Li says my kind of innovation deserves more of a reward. Not only did he want to meet me, but he arranged for me to throw out the first pitch at a home game.

The day of, we wait inside the door leading to the dugout. Fu Li's not as tall as my dad. I lean toward him and try to sniff without being too obvious. Not rain and coffee. Fu Li smells like baseball: bleached uniform and glove oil. Nothing will ever be exactly like Dad, but Fu Li smells okay too.

I wonder if he gets frustrated with not having a bubble for being Mexinese, but he looks pretty well adjusted for a grown-up. We walk into the dugout, and the people around the surrounding railing above us cheer.

"Ready?" Fu Li pulls out a packet of dehydrated ginger. It's the same kind Grandma buys from the Asian grocery store. Maybe his grandma makes him chew it when his belly is upset too. He offers me a piece, and I take it.

"Thanks." I shove it into my inner cheek.

"So, I heard about how you raised the money," he says. "Not a square dancing fan?"

I shrug. "I guess it isn't as bad as I thought in the beginning."

"Yeah, everyone has to square dance at some point." His eye twitches and I wonder who he had to dance with. "Anyway, thanks to you, eighty kids who couldn't afford to play ball are going to be starting Little League next season."

I never thought about it that way and realize how lucky I am. I just hope one of those kids loves baseball as much as I do.

Fu Li tips his cap. "You know, it was never about the grades, Lupe."

I think of the note he gave Uncle Hector to give to me. *Anyone can pitch a good inning, pitching an entire good game takes character.*

251

"It was about making the effort to do something you were always capable of," he says. "What you did instead showed more character than getting grades."

I shuffle my cleat on the ground. I might be as red as the dirt.

I stare out at the mound that's fourteen feet further than I'm used to. "What if I don't make it to the plate?"

"You will. You're a kid who makes things happen." He puts his hand on my shoulder. "Besides, you've been working toward this for a long time."

We stand at the edge of the dugout. A deep voice like the guys on the radio station fills the air. "Tonight, throwing out the first pitch, is Guadalupe Wong of Issaquaaaaaaah!"

I chew harder on the ginger and pick at the ties on my mitt.

Fu Li leads me up the stairs to the top of the dugout, and we wait. The crowd sees us and starts chanting, "Fu Li! Fu Li! Fu Li!" If I squint my ears, I can almost hear, "Lupe! Lupe! . . ."

He holds out a hand and my heart leaps. Is this his secret handshake?

Suddenly, the cheers are drowned out by a techno beat and music. Fiddles screech out, and a voice with a heavy Southern accent wails, "Where did you come from, where did you go, where did you come from, Cotton-Eye Joe?" I can't believe what I'm hearing.

Fu Li winks at me and pushes his hand even closer. "Ready to do this, Lupe?'

"What did you—" I croak out, taking a tiny step back. "Now?"

252

He takes my mitt and puts it on the top of my head. "Let's show 'em how it's done."

I shake my tingly hands out at my sides. "Okay, but I lead."

He laughs and pulls his arm back. I bow and hold out my hand. He curtsies and takes it. We promenade from the dugout, kicking our feet together in sync. The cheers of the crowd are so loud I can barely make out the tune.

I glance up to where Mom and Paolo are supposed to be sitting above the dugout.

But they're not sitting. They're dancing too.

A few guys are stumbling around in sloppy do-si-dos.

I spin Fu Li and he laughs. We dance toward the mound.

"Where did you come from, where did you go. Where did you come from, Cotton-Eye Joe?" twangs again.

Fu Li smiles at me, and I see it. Just like in the picture where my dad's holding the crab. I see the tiny wrinkles around Fu Li's eyes too. Standing right there on the mound . . . I remember.

My dad was no quitter. Fu Li's smile is like Dad's the first time I whistled. The same smile when I finger-painted my entire face and body. It's the same smile when he would dance with Mom in the kitchen. And it's the same smile he had when I hit my first baseball. I know Fu Li's not Dad, but . . .

I remember.

I fight back the tears that are blurring my vision. This is even better than a secret handshake and hug.

Fu Li takes my glove off my head and hands it to me, smiling.

"Now throw some heat." He turns and jogs toward home plate to catch.

My dad is standing right beside me. I can almost feel him rustle my hair. *Well, we got here together, didn't we, Lupe?* He steps aside to give me the room I need to play on the field he never got to.

I whisper to myself, "Center your weight on the rubber. Be deliberate in your windup . . ."

Even as I swallow ginger, trying not to cry, the crowd yells louder.

It's not as perfect as when I'll be the first Chinacan or Mexinese girl throwing a no-hitter on this field.

But it's pretty close.

ACKNOWLEDGMENTS

I am so thankful for many who in some way either supported me or helped Lupe's story enter the world.

First among them are Mom and Dad—Everything you taught me makes its way into my writing. I try to follow your example daily to love everyone, judge no one, and just be kind. Mom, I am forever grateful I was able to read this book to you and make you laugh a little before you left.

To the love of my life, Mark. How on Earth among billions did I find my perfect partner in life, gardening, growing old, and writing?! You are my perfect person. God help our children as we get older!

My Elena and Sophia: You are precious to me and inspire me daily in life and writing. Elena, your spitfire nature and tenacity will take you far in life. I just always want to be on your side.

Sophia, your kind heart and beautiful soul will serve you well in life. You are both powerful, intelligent, lovely humans. How lucky I am to be your mom!

My new kids, Bethany and Max, you make me proud and happy every day. I know sometimes the parents we end up with aren't the ones we expected, but I am having a blast being yours. I love you both so much.

My sister Melissa and cousins (Tom, Steve, Angie, and Rob), who made my childhood ridiculous, loving, and full of ideas to write about.

My best friend, Mai Nguyen—We don't need many. Just one. So glad I have you.

There are many kinds of family. And now I have another. My writing family:

The Papercuts: Cindy Roberts, Mark Maciejewski, Maggie Adams, Eli Isenberg, David Colburn, Jason Hine, Angie Lewis. What an eclectic group we are. I appreciate the weekly honesty and support we give each other's work. I'd forfeit my color-coded critique pens for you guys!

NICK THOMAS! Wow . . . what a strange meeting and magical journey. I am so grateful for your insight into making this novel richer and more heartfelt. You have taught me so much and done so with kindness and truth. I have thoroughly enjoyed this journey with you, friend! Not only are you an editor extraordinaire, you are a brave and thoughtful man. Onward!

Allison Remcheck—You are a novel-whisperer and I am so thankful to have you for my agent, and now friend. You are what every writer dreams of discovering in someone to champion their work.

Thank you to my agency family at Stimola Literary Studio: Rosemary, Peter, Allison H. for supporting me. You are the backbone for so many!

Thank you to all those at Levine Querido for giving Lupe a chance to chat with the world. Arthur A. Levine, what a solid family and gracious home you've created! Thank you so much for your guiding words and for being an advocate for voices that need to be heard. And huge gratitude to the rest of the team: Publicity Manager Alexandra Hernandez, Marketing Director Antonio Gonzalez Cerna, and Assistant Editor Meghan Maria McCullough for all the behind the scenes work you've all done for me and my book. You are one hard working group! Thank you for all you do and for your support. Go team LQ!

Mason London, thank you for creating the cover art for Lupe which is far better than I could have ever envisioned. You truly captured Lupe's spirit!

Anamika Bhatnagar for catching errors and fixing details. You are pretty magical!

Huge thanks to Maeve Norton, who designed this book. And Leslie Cohen and Freesia Blizard in Production at Chronicle Books, thank you for making this book so beautiful!

The Society for Childrens Book Writers and Illustrators

(SCBWI)—There is no way to extend enough gratitude for all you've given me during this journey. Some of my favorite people in my life I've met because of you.

Las Musas, thank for creating a welcoming, lovely community of escritoras. Your support and hermandad has been full of warmth in my writing world.

Marissa Graff for sitting on my shoulder spouting editorial wisdom. I am so grateful to have met you along this literary road.

To my writing mentor, Gloria Kempton, my guru in teaching me to ask the right questions to bring characters and story to life.

Thank you to my beta readers who read Lupe's story and helped to make it better. Melissa Koosman, Rob Vlock, Angela Albrecht, Rob Forsberg, Sophia Chow.

To my online critique partners along the way whose tough writing love made me a better writer: Hiromi Cota, Orlyn Carney, Birgitte Necessary, Pam Fulton, Fred Campagnoli, Patti Albaugh, Maribeth Durst.

To Connor, reader extraordinaire, for your perspective and feelings on making sure Niles was authentic to how you feel. I did my best to listen. You are already a cool young man, and are going to be a really cool grown-up.

And to Liz LaFebre for expert insight and for introducing me to Connor.

Lyn Miller-Lachmann, thank you for your expertise, feedback and taking time to help another writer learn. And might I fan-girl a bit. You are an amazing writer and storyteller!

260

My teachers: Mr. and Mrs. Presho, Mrs. Arnoldus, Mrs. Griffin, and Uncle Ted—In some way you all encouraged me in the love of reading and books. There is no more precious gift you could have given a kid to discover a huge world beyond a tiny desert town. Thank you.

Coach Jeannette Montgomery, Coach David Montgomery, and Dad. You encouraged love of the game, discipline, and hard work.

And dear Reader, thanks for reading! If I could send you a private message that I hope this book imparts, this is it: Whatever you are, be that. Be your most sincere, unique, beautiful self. And as a boy in a book once said, "If you're the real you, the right people will love you."

ABOUT THE AUTHOR

Donna Barba Higuera grew up dodging dust devils in the oil-fields of Central California. She has spent her entire life blending folklore with her experiences into stories that fill her imagination. Now she weaves them to write picture books and novels.

Donna eventually traded the dust of Central California for the mists of the Pacific Northwest. She lives there with her husband, four children, three dogs, and ~~three~~ two frogs. She is currently working on her debut picture book and next middle-grade novel.

You can find her online at www.dbhiguera.com.

THE LANTERNS PAPERBACKS DESIGN

The design of Lantern Paperbacks was originated by Filip Peraić. He says: "The Lantern Paperbacks needed a visual identity which symbolizes their beautiful mission of 'spreading light into the world.' This brief was brought to life through a colorful line look, led by our special 'L' mark, formed by nine rays of light."

**Lantern
Paperbacks**

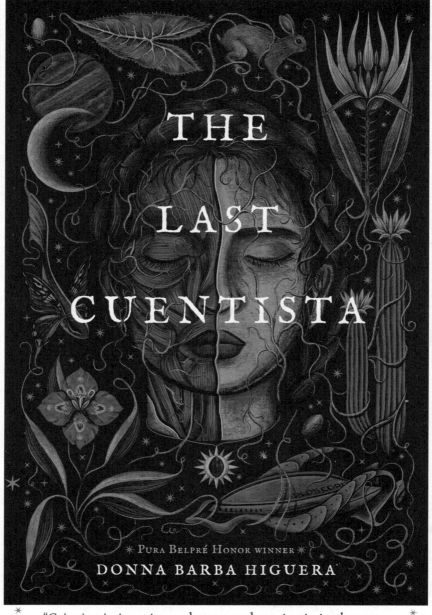

THE
LAST
CUENTISTA

✳ Pura Belpré Honor winner ✳

DONNA BARBA HIGUERA